I AM THE NIGHT

THE NIGHT FIRM 3

KARPOV KINRADE

To the Demon Turk for snapping the whip and for seeing my heart and loving me. This book wouldn't be here right now without you.

CONTENTS

THE TREE

The caged bird sings
with a fearful trill
of things unknown
but longed for still
and his tune is heard
on the distant hill
for the caged bird
sings of freedom.
~Maya Angelou, Caged Bird

A VAST CANVAS of emerald green stretches before us, dotted with colorful wildflowers, towering trees, moss covered boulders, bushes and plants and all manner of nature. The day is warm, and a cool breeze teases my skin. Sebastian rests his hands on my shoulders and uses his strong fingers to rub the knots of tension out of my muscles. I lean into him, closing my eyes, enjoying the feel of him at my back as he massages me. The scent of wildflowers carries on the wind, and I breathe it all in and smile.

"You've been at this for hours," he says, his lips brushing my earlobe as he speaks. "Ready for a break?"

I open my eyes and look around, then sigh. "There's still too much to do," I say. "The people need food. What good is this new expanse of Otherworld Ava'Kara gave her life to create if it's not livable?"

In the wake of what happened nearly a month ago, I thought things would be easier for the magical folk who claimed this new land as their home. It didn't take long to realize the world expansion created new problems. There were no homes, no farms, no food sources. It was an untamed wilderness that was created raw and uninhabitable by anyone but woodland creatures and dryads.

And few of us had the kind of magic needed to make this part of the world more hospitable. Which means for the past several weeks, the Night brothers, Lily, and myself have been working tirelessly to cultivate this new land for those displaced.

For many long days after that night, I feared my magic would never return. I was more exhausted than I'd ever been in my life. Even the revelation that I was one of the Fates returned couldn't penetrate the fog that surrounded me. I spent most of that time unconscious.

Callia, the unicorn I inadvertently pulled into this world, disappeared shortly after telling me I was one of the Fates reincarnated. For a time I was convinced I hallucinated her.

The brothers nursed me back to health with Liam and Matilda's disgusting potions, Sebastian's back rubs, Derek's wry jokes to make me laugh, and Elijah's gentle voice reading to me when I couldn't keep my eyes open long enough to read for myself. I snuggled Liam's baby, cuddled in front of the fire on long nights, listened to Liam playing his violin, and I soaked in the love and affection offered to me. I tried hard not to think about Cole, but his ghost haunted me. It's now impossible to feel like we are a complete family without him.

I glance down at my ring, his ring, and twist it on my finger, a melancholy settling over me. Sebastian notices and pulls me tighter into an embrace, his arms circling my waist as I lay my head against his chest and settle my hands over his heart.

He kisses the top of my head and sighs. "I think about him too."

"He belongs with us," I say, sadly.

Sebastian doesn't respond. I know it's complicated for him. For all of the Night brothers. They feel guilt and anger in equal measure. I have no guilt, but somehow my anger is dimmed. Despite the fact that Cole betrayed me in such a heinous way, taking the form of my twin brother, convincing me Adam was not only still alive but had committed monstrous acts of violence against the innocent,*I can't help but think of all that he has gone through that led him up to that moment and forgive him.* Cole is a man tortured by his past, both by acts done to him as well as those he himself has committed out of anger and vengeance. Did his brothers deserve his wrath? Perhaps. But justice without mercy becomes tainted by its own misguided righteousness. We need the tempering influence of compassion and forgiveness, otherwise we risk perpetuating a self-destructive cycle that can only end badly for everyone.

I could stay angry at him forever. He would deserve it, if that's how we are meant to measure justice. But if I consider what he's been through, where he came from, what his life cost him... it's harder to stay angry. Perspective shapes our perception of life. And his story gives me a different perspective of his actions. They have to be seen together. His choices don't exist in a vacuum. We are, all of us, stories told and retold with layers that cannot be ignored if we want the truth of a thing. So who can possibly measure the weight of a person's soul? Who among us can ever truly know what another deserves?

I choose to believe we all deserve forgiveness. Mercy. Love. Compassion. Perspective.

I can offer that to Cole at least.

I can't yet offer it to Jerry, but someday maybe I'll

be able to see the brokenness in him and forgive him for what he did to me as well as to Mary and her child.

Near us, something explodes, sending dirt and rock flying through the air. Sebastian attempts to shield me with his body, but I use my power to subdue the debris, letting it fall harmlessly back to the ground with ease.

He shakes his head, grinning, his forest green eyes sparkling. His wild, dark hair is dusted with specks of dirt, and his simple shirt clings to his broad chest and shoulders, muscles rippling under the stretched fabric. He's like a sculpture carved from the very earth. He's definitely in his element here. "I'm still not used to how powerful you've become since the spell you performed."

"Neither am I," I say. "But it feels good. I can tell there's still so much untapped in me that I want to explore."

"Slowly," he says. "Don't push yourself too hard. We still don't know what you being a Fate means or how it will impact your abilities, your health, or even your life span."

I roll my eyes. This has been a constant discussion since my powers returned. Once I was well enough to get about on my own, I accidentally blew up the kitchen trying to light the fire. We all realized then that not only had I not lost my powers, but I had unlocked them to the nth degree. They flooded me in a dizzying avalanche of magic I am slowly learning to control.

That's when Callia returned. She showed up after

the explosion and smiled widely. "I've been waiting for you to wake up and recover your strength," she said. "I'm here to train you, as I have trained all the Fates before you."

"You'll teach me how to use my powers?" I asked, stunned.

But then everyone looked at me strangely. "This is Callia," I told them, gesturing to her, but she shook her head.

"They cannot see me. Only you. While you have brought my spirit back, my body is no longer viable."

And so I had to explain to the Night brothers that I had an invisible unicorn to train me.

There was some concern I'd done damage to my brain after the spell, but Elijah was the first to point out that the Fates have always been able to see what others couldn't. He felt it made sense, so the others backed off. They're still wigged out by it though, I can tell.

It was actually Callia's idea to use my powers to cultivate this land, and it was a brilliant one. Not only am I doing good, but it's a practical way to stretch and test what I can do.

Everyday I'm gaining discipline under the scrutinizing eyes of the brothers and the fleeting attentions of Callia who comes and goes at her whim.

Liam strolls over, a huge grin on his face, his golden eyes flashing and his auburn red hair in sexy disarray. His simple trousers and sleeveless shirt are tinged with burn marks. "Sorry about that. I was trying something new and it got a bit out of control."

"Let me guess. You thought blowing shit up would be a faster way to get the job done?" A smile tugs at my lips and Liam grins sheepishly.

"Maybe," he says.

"Did it work?" Sebastian asks.

"Not really." Liam shrugs and we all laugh.

I reluctantly pull out of Sebastian's embrace and crack my knuckles. "Alright, boys, back to work. These trees won't move themselves."

Sebastian groans and I clap my hands together and close my eyes, re-centering myself in my power. I tug on the chord of earth magic I need and carefully release it, moving it into the roots of the great conifer before me. This is a delicate process, uprooting an old growth and replanting it. Initially I destroyed several trees, but the dryads performed a transformation ceremony for them so we could use them to build houses and tools instead. Still, we've been trying to save as much of nature as we could. Like this beauty before me.

I can hear the tree speaking to my soul and I realize it doesn't want to move. It likes its spot just fine, thank you very much.

I frown. *Would you be willing to reshape yourself? To become shelter for a family in need? I ask through a mental connection that has formed between us.*

We are cleaning this particular area for housing.

This has been our work for a few weeks now. Using my combination of elemental magic along with each of the brothers' unique skills, we have been uprooting and moving trees, plowing fields, laying foundations for housing, paving roads, and creating infrastructures for a new town.

The tree considers my request, and I send it images of the people I'm trying to help. The children who will laugh and dance and play here, the mothers who will nurse their children, and the parents who will nourish their families, who will work the land to grow and thrive.

The tree agrees to a transformation, and I have to think fast, as I haven't tried anything like this before.

"Change of plans," I say as I grab my bag and pull out my sketch book. I quickly draw an idea forming in my mind. I study the structure of the tree to create the body of the home, and as I do, another consciousness tugs at me.

The tree, sensing my thoughts, helps me form an image of what it would like to be. It has a grand trunk, large enough to drive several carriages through, and it wants to expand, to be even grander.

In surprise, I realize it wants to connect to the tree near it, to bond with her, to create something with her, so I stretch my magic and seek her permission for this plan.

She agrees, and somehow this spell becomes something more. A partnership. A marriage of a kind. Their roots have been touching, connected, and now they will become one.

Callia appears beside me, as suddenly as she always does. "This is a wonderful test of your magic," she says, delighted. Her ebony skin shines like liquid and her silver eyes practically glow as she instructs me. "You'll need to use all of your elements for this. Air and Earth to help shape. Fire to burn away what's not needed and water to temper and strengthen what is. Light to give it life and Darkness to strip that which no longer serves. For in any transformation, there is death. We cannot give birth to new life, to new forms, without it."

I sigh but nod. I still have a hard time using the Darkness within me without worrying it will corrupt my soul, but I know I must embrace all the elements for there to be true balance.

I reach for Sebastian and Liam's hands and grip them hard, pulling their power into me as well.

We all work better when we are together, we have found.

Cole pushes into my memories, and I shake off the thought of what our family could be if he were here to complete it. I can't think of him right now, I must focus.

Exhaling, I release my magic into the trees and their roots expand as they twist and reshape, growing in new directions, intertwining as they form themselves into a new kind of creation that so far only exists in my sketchbook.

Sweat beads on my lip. Heat pulses in me. I feel Elijah and Derek approach. I sense when they take their brothers' hands, forming a circle, sending me more magic, more power.

The energy within me builds and builds and is expelled in a wave of magic that pulses out of us all and into the ground, the trees, and the air around us. The earth shakes and cracks as the wind rises, whipping my hair into my face.

I grip Sebastian and Liam's hands harder to preserve our connection.

And when the earth and wind settle, when the magic retreats back into me, I open my eyes and gasp.

Before us stands a beautiful new house, an organic and living structure made from the trees themselves, with gently curved walls and a sloped roof twined with vines.

"How did you do that?" a voice behind us asks.

I turn to see Lily looking on in awe.

"I don't know," I say, releasing my death grip on the brothers and stretching my sore fingers. "The trees helped."

Lily smiles, and it lights up her face. "They are so happy. None of us have ever seen anything like this."

She runs a hand through her hot pink hair—the new color of the week— and looks around, stunned. "The others want this too. The entire grove wants to be made into houses," she says. "Except that one," she says, pointing to one off to the side. "He would like to be moved closer to the water. He's thirsty."

I laugh. "I think that can be arranged."

The Night brothers are still silent, staring at the house we just created, then staring at me with stunned expressions.

Liam pulls me against his chest and brushes a lock of hair out of my face. His golden eyes are full of admiration and awe. "You amaze me," he says, and before I can respond he leans in and claims my lips with his. A spark ignites between us, as it always does when we touch, and I lose myself in the softness of his lips and the hardness of his body pressed against mine.

His tongue teases my bottom lip, and I moan in desire as need flares in me.

But before we set the forest on fire, I pull away, panting.

He releases me reluctantly with a wicked grin. "Later, we will finish what we started."

I flush red and sigh again, wishing later was now.

Instead I turn to the home we just helped build and step through the impressive French doors making up the entrance. Not only have the trees formed this structure, but they have furnished it as well. A table, counters, chairs, bed frames, all made from the living trees. It's incredible.

Derek steps next to me and slips an arm around my waist. The Water Druid always has a calming effect on me. And though he's been working just as hard as all of us, he's managed to stay much cleaner. His close-cropped dark hair is still neat and tidy. His button-up shirt and pants dust free. I don't know how he manages it. He glances down at me with his sapphire eyes and smiles. "You've truly surpassed yourself."

My magic is still radiating out of me as I look up to him. "Do you think Lyx'Ara and her people will like it?"

"They will love it," Derek promises.

The Light Dragon lives with her people, and has been foraging the forests helping them make ends meet since the world's expansion. Some have died without proper shelter and food, thus creating the urgent need for a town, for protection, and for sustenance. She asked us for help and we were happy to offer it, though it meant putting nearly all of our legal work on hold.

Derek has handled a few minor cases as needed, but mostly we have been here, all day, every day, working tirelessly to create a new world.

"Sebastian is right, this would be a good time for a break. We should give Lyx a report on our progress and let her know about this," I say, waving a free hand at the house we just helped create. "This will change how we approach the rest of the development."

I look around, frowning. "Come to think of it, I'm surprised she hasn't been here today, yet."

"She has a lot going on," Derek says, pragmatically. "But I know she will be happy to hear what you've accomplished today."

"We," I clarify. "What we've accomplished. I couldn't have done this—any of this—alone."

As we head to the carriage, it begins to rain, and a flash buzzes in my brain, giving me a low grade headache.

We were already headed to see Lyx, but now I know, we must hurry. I just don't know why.

THE DRAGON

Do not stand at my grave and weep
I am not there; I do not sleep.
I am a thousand winds that blow,
I am the diamond glints on snow,
~Mary Elizabeth Frye, Do Not Stand at My Grave
and Weep

MY HEART HAMMERS in my chest in excitement as we head to the carriage. Lily rides up front to drive and the five of us pile into the back.

It's a bumpy trip to the Light Dragon's home base, and not one particularly suited for a horse and buggy, but it's the easiest way for all of us to travel. I make a mental note that we should pave some roads along this path soon. For everyone's sake.

While I didn't know Lyx well before, working with

her these past few weeks has brought us closer. Even her relationship with the Night brothers has mended as we all worked side by side to build her and her people a new home. I've witnessed her devotion to Ava'Kara's baby, watching as she has cared for the dragon child as her own. I've seen her dedication to her people, tireless and unconditional. She gets her hands dirty, working with us day in and day out. At night, after a long day, we will sit with her around a camp fire, stew cooking over the flames in a cast iron pot, as we shared stories, made music, formed friendships.

This work has been immensely fulfilling, and it's largely thanks to the Light Dragon and her vision for what could be. I can't wait to tell her what's now possible, thanks to the trees willingness to transform themselves. It's truly a game changer.

The carriage wheel hits a stone and wobbles to one side, but Elijah uses his wind magic to help it stay righted as we hastily continue our journey.

We stop abruptly and I lurch forward into Derek's lap, who catches me with a cheeky grin. "If you wanted to get closer, all you had to do was ask." He winks and helps me exit the carriage with some manner of dignity left.

His flirtatious smile lingers as we look around for Lyx.

We have come to a hidden cove carved into the side of a massive mountain. The shore is covered in a carpet of mossy green, dotted with brilliant yellow flowers that lead to a glassy clear stretch of water being fed by a tall waterfall crashing off the jagged rocks of the mountain.

But a scream catches in my throat when I look at the water more closely.

Floating face up is Lyx'Ara, her eyes open, a wound in her chest oozing a viscous purple.

"Lyx!" I scream and run to the edge of the water, using my magic to pull her to shore.

"Is that... her blood?" I whisper, unable to pull my eyes away. She practically glows in the water, her Light magic clinging to her and giving me some hope that despite all evidence to the contrary, she might still be okay.

"Yes," Elijah says. "Dragons bleed purple."

With tears stinging my eyes, I step into the lake and reach for her, pulling her to shore. Her blood stains my clothes and my hands, but I don't care. Once on land, I check her vital signs to no avail.

"Liam, help her!" I scream.

Liam is already by my side, examining her as thoroughly and carefully as he can, his face hard, his eyes serious.

Finally he looks up. "She's... dead."

"She... she can't be," I say, too astonished to form a clear thought. "That makes no sense. Try again!"

Liam shakes his head. "I'm sorry. But... it looks like someone murdered her."

"How?" I demand. "How can you even kill a

dragon? I thought they were immortal? The most powerful beings in the world."

Elijah kneels beside us, examining her himself. "They are. And the only thing that can kill a dragon... is another dragon," he says.

"There's no murder weapon on her body," Derek says. "But it appears she was killed by a puncture to her chest from something cylindrical in shape with a very sharp tip."

"And her soul hasn't departed," Elijah says. "It should have."

"What do you mean?" I ask. I'm trying hard not to hyperventilate. My hands are still stained with her blood. I've still got her head in my lap.

"When a dragon dies, it's thought their souls depart and their bodies turn to magic and dissipate, putting themselves back into the universe to live again," Elijah says. "But her soul is still attached to her body, and she clearly hasn't turned to magic."

"Have you ever seen a dragon die?" I ask softly.

The brothers all shake their heads. "No one has," Sebastian says. "Except you."

He looks at me and I realize he's right. I was there when Ava'Kara died. And she did disappear into magic, though I assumed that was a byproduct of the spell, not the standard MO for magical spontaneous dragon cremation.

"We need to get Ifi and Elal here," I say to no one in particular.

Lily nods. "I can go. I don't need a carriage."

I'm about to ask how, but she's gone before I get the words out.

I return my focus to the Light Dragon and run my hands over her eyes, closing them. Even in death she is just as beautiful, with her silver hair and inner glow. It's then that I notice she's clutching something in her hand. I pry it open and find her signet ring within. I take it to study, wondering if this was some kind of clue about her killer. Why was she holding it instead of wearing it?

Knowing how the justice system works here—which is not well—I pocket it, hoping to uncover any secrets it might hold, and then look around. "Where's the baby?"

Liam glances at me, frowning. "That's an excellent question."

"We need to find her before whoever killed Lyx does. Maybe they were after the child?" The thought makes me sick, but I know I can't afford to overlook this possibility. Ava'Kara tasked me with looking after her heir until she came of age, and I will be damned if I don't do everything in my power to honor her last wishes.

Ava'Zara, the daughter and air to the Water Dragon, has grown more than expected in the weeks we've been working with Lyx. The child mostly stays in dragon form, but every so often she'll change to her more human form, I suspect to marvel at it. But she seems to prefer being a dragon, and who wouldn't, if I'm being honest.

"Maybe they already have the child," Sebastian says darkly.

"I refuse to believe that," I say, as I gently move Lyx off my lap and onto the mossy ground so I can look for the child.

"Zara?" I call out to her softly, hoping she's nearby. The brothers join the searching, looking for clues, making notes about the crime scene.

As I look for the baby, Callia's training comes back to me. "Use your magic to amplify your senses," she would tell me. "You are so much more powerful than you realize."

So I do. I close my eyes and dig deep into myself, into the well of elemental power that lives within me, and I gently tug at a string. Another trick Callia taught me. To braid the elements into a string that I can use when I need a little bit of all six of my abilities.

My skin tingles as the magic dances over me, as if it's lighting me up. I send the string out, imbuing it with myself, with my senses. What it sees, I see. What it hears or feels, I hear and feel. And that is how I sense the presence of Zara, hiding behind the waterfall deep within the cave. She's scared. And she's not alone.

"I've found her," I announce to the guys, who all approach me. "She's close, but someone is with her."

Sebastian moves to leave. "Stay here, I'll be back."

I grab his arm. "We go together. I'm no damsel in distress, remember?"

As if to prove my point, I raise my arms and as I do, the water before us parts, revealing the bottom of the pool and a path straight to the waterfall. Even Derek—the Water Druid himself—looks impressed, and we all walk forward, each of us on alert. We don't know what we'll find in the cave. Someone helping the child, or the person who killed Lyx.

My fingers ignite with flames as my protective instincts flare up, and Liam looks at my hands and shows me his. He's got a fireball ready.

I nod and we continue. The waterfall parts for us at my command and I guide the brothers past the damp entrance into the depth of the cave that divides into tunnels leading in several directions.

"Which way?" Sebastian asks, his muscles tense, his jaw clenched. All four of them look on edge, and I'm sure I look the same.

I close my eyes and pull on that thread of power again, letting it guide me. "To the left," I say, pointing.

The cave is musty and wet, and everything I step on makes a dead kind of squishy sound that makes my skin crawl.

I hear a tiny roar, like that of a baby dragon, and I move faster, using the fire in my hands as flashlights to see. The others don't need it, they can see fine in the dark.

The tunnel expands into an open space with crystals hanging from the ceiling and a small pond of muddy water in the center. A tiny blue dragon floats in the water, making playful growling sounds and spitting water from her mouth as she practices her dragon gifts.

"Zara!" She looks up at me and makes a cute chirping noise, then flaps her wings and awkwardly flies to my arms, landing heavily against my chest, soaking me with mud and water. But I don't care. I'm too relieved that she's unharmed. She nuzzles her head against my chest and I hold her more tightly as I look around.

"I know you're here," I say to the other person hiding in the cave. "You can come out now. We're not going to hurt you."

I wait a moment, the silence deafening, but I caution the brothers to stay still with a sharp glance. If we make a ruckus, the person won't come out.

Finally, a small shuffling sound alerts us to the presence of a young girl. She is soaking wet and looks about nine or ten years old. She wears rags that stick to her frail, bone thin body, her dirty blond hair caked with grime and clinging to a face that looks sunken in from hunger. Tears streak her skin, creating trails as they clear off the dirt from her cheeks.

I kneel down to her level. "What's your name?" I ask in my softest voice. The child looks like a wild animal ready to bolt at the slightest hint of danger.

"Ana," she says.

"What are you doing in here?" Sebastian asks, his

voice gruff, and she shies back, sinking into the shadows around her.

"Sebastian, she's scared. Use your gentle voice." I reprimand.

I hand him the dragon, who curls up in his arms happily, and take small steps towards the girl. "I'm Eve," I say. "I'm a friend of Lyx. Were you her friend too?"

From the shadows I see her small head bob. "I tried to save her," she says softly.

My heart leaps at that. "Did you see what happened to Lyx?" I ask. "Who hurt her?"

The girl shakes her head, and my heart plummets. If only it had been that easy. "I was taking Zara for a walk. Lyx let's me help with the baby sometimes." She puffs out her chest, clearly proud of her trusted standing with the Light Dragon. "We got back and she was floating in the water, bleeding. I went to her, and she looked at me, like she was okay. But, but she was scared. She said to go, to... " She hesitates, her lower lip quivering. "To take the baby and hide. Then the light went out of her eyes and I ran in here with Zara. I... " She sniffles. "I didn't know what else to do."

The child begins sobbing, and I close the distance between us and pull her into my arms, holding her close. She cries on my shoulder until her tears are used up, then sniffles and wipes her face with the back of her hand. "Is it my fault?" she asks in a voice that cracks my heart open.

"No, love, it's not your fault. You did the right thing. You saved Zara."

Liam clears his throat. "We need to leave. Once word spreads, Enforcers will be here."

Shit.

"We have to get Zara out of here before they arrive. I don't trust anyone else to take her right now."

Derek looks like he's about to argue, but I stand firm. "She's coming with us, until we know what happened. All I know for sure is that none of us killed Lyx, so we are the only ones I trust at the moment."

I take Ana's hand and lead her out of the cave. "Where are your parents?" I ask.

She shrugs. "Don't got none. Lyx took care of me."

Double shit.

"Would you like to come home with us? At least until we can find you a proper home."

Derek frowns again, but says nothing. Smart man.

The girl looks at the brothers, then back at me, and slowly nods.

"Good, let's get out of here and we'll show you the castle we live in. You're going to love it."

The girl's eyes widen as I once again part the waters so we can cross back to land. "How'd you do that?" she asks.

"It's part of my powers," I say. Then I point to our carriage. "I need you to go get in there okay? We'll be right behind you."

She reluctantly releases my hand and does as

instructed, petting the horses on the way, and I approach the Night brothers. Sebastian still has the baby dragon in his arms.

"We shouldn't take the kids with us," Derek says, frowning. "It's a bad idea on so many levels."

"I know," I say, "but what choice do we have? Ana has nowhere to go. She's skin and bones as it is, plus she may have witnessed the murder, or at least seen more than she remembers. And Zara's life could be in danger. We don't know why Lyx was killed or how, so we have to assume the baby dragon's a target until we learn more. And that means hiding her from the Enforcers and especially the dragons."

Liam shifts, his posture still on alert. "I agree with Eve. We can't leave them behind."

Elijah shrugs. "It would be fascinating to learn more about the behaviors and habits of a newly hatched dragon. So little is known about them given how rare they are in general."

Derek sighs and looks to Sebastian for support, but Zara purrs against his chest, snuggled tight and looking quite content. The Earth Druid shrugs and I smile at the scene of him looking so nurturing.

"You all realize we could lose our license to practice law for this, right?" asks Derek.

"Maybe it's time we found a new calling anyways," Liam says, surprising us all.

"You don't want to be a lawyer anymore?" I ask.

"I didn't say that," he says, "but when you are

immortal, it does well to change things up a bit from time to time. I've been thinking a lot about the past and what our future might hold. I'm just not sure I want to spend too many more years at this."

Derek looks beyond exasperated, but shakes his head. "We can't have this conversation right now. We have to go. Particularly if we are kidnapping two children."

"We are," I confirm, smiling at the baby dragon and trying not to look at Lyx's body lying by the water. "We should go." But we don't leave right away. Without exchanging words, we all pause before the water and stand in silence moment. In honor of Lyx's life, in mourning of her death. Then we turn to the carriage.

Derek, still annoyed with all of our plans, sits up front to. Liam joins him, leaving me in the back with the two kids, Sebastian and Elijah.

The plan is to head straight to the castle and to avoid any confrontation on the way.

But, that plan is shit upon within fifteen minutes of driving.

The steady rainfall that began earlier turns into a full scale storm, cracking the sky open and shifting the earth in its power and force. Everyone looks at me, but I shrug. "I'm not doing this."

The horses neigh in panic, pulling against each other and toppling our carriage to the side.

Sebastian clutches the dragon, and I reach for Ana,

holding her close and cocooning us in a ball of air to cushion our fall.

Still, we land hard, and I know I'll have bruises tomorrow to tell this tale.

Liam rushes to help pull Ana out of the carriage just as a fire ball lands a few feet away, singeing the earth and nearly incinerating us.

The baby dragon hiccups and a stream of water flows out of her mouth, quenching the flames, but another fire ball hits to our right and Ana screams and hides behind me.

"What the hell is happening?" I shout, using my magic to quench the fires as fast as they appear.

The wind is a frenzied thing, whipping around us as flames continue to rain from the sky and burn the earth. I look up and see them. Two giant dragons fighting amidst the thunderous clouds. I recognize the red one. Dath'Racul, the Fire Dragon. But the other is new to me. It's a pale blue dragon with shimmering white scales around its face. "That's the Air Dragon?" I ask.

Elijah nods. "Ventus'Arak. He and Dath'Racul don't always see eye to eye."

I snort. "That's pretty clear."

Through the wind we can hear them speaking... or rather shouting at each other. "You killed her!" Ventus says.

Racul roars, sending another fire ball flaming through the sky. "I did no such thing."

"If not you, then who? You always hated her for leaving the Council," Arak says.

"That does not mean I killed her," he bellows.

Two more dragons fly up. One a deep green and the other dark as pitch. Ra'Terr, the Darkness Dragon, I recognize as the one who guards the prison. But I've never seen the earth dragon before. She's magnificent. Her scales sparkle under the Dragon's Breath and look like emeralds shining in the sky.

"That's Brock'Mir," Elijah says. "And this is what remains of the Dragon Council," he says with sadness in his voice. "To lose two dragons so close together is a true tragedy for our world."

"Brothers, cease this bickering. We must work together to find out who killed our sister," Brock'Mir says, but they ignore her and continue fighting, shaking the earth and splitting the sky with their fury.

I fear their wrath will not end until another dragon has been killed, very likely taking us with them.

"We need to get out of here," I shout, as I survey the damaged, overturned carriage.

Pulling on my power, I use the wind to right the wagon, setting it back on its wheels, but still it tilts to one side since one of them are broken. The horses are still in a panic, and I approach them cautiously, infusing myself with light as I pour peace into them. They calm quickly, despite the tumultuous storm still raging around us.

I pat one on the nose, murmuring reassuringly to them.

Before I can figure out how to fix the wheel and get us back on the road, the Dragon's Breath above us begins to shimmer and stretch, a tear appearing in the fabric of the world itself, revealing a true wonder. A dragon, the largest I've ever seen—easily three times the size of the others, flies through the tear and hovers in the air. Her wings are stretched wide and she is covered in golden scales that glow like the sun. She lowers herself to earth, shifting into human form as she does, until a woman stands there, long hair golden and wavy, an intricate golden crown on her head, and golden wings draped over her back like a cloak. Her skin is iridescent and shines brightly and her eyes are golden orbs. She wears a gown that shimmers with flecks of gold that catch in the light, and her presence causes all of the dragons to stop their arguing and land before her, turning back to their human form even as they bow before her.

"Who's that?" I whisper to Elijah, whose jaw has dropped in amazement.

"That... the gods help us, that is Amir'Amora'Akar. The Mother of Dragons."

THE MOTHER

Out of the ash
  I rise with my red hair
  And I eat men like air.'
  ~Slyvia Plath, Lady Lazarus

I'M MOMENTARILY PARALYZED by the wonder of her, but then, as Elijah attempts to pull me into a curtsy, I take Ana's hand and usher her back into the carriage which wobbles with her weight but doesn't tip over.

"Stay in here and stay hidden," I whisper, and I take the baby dragon from Sebastian and hand her to the girl. "And keep Zara hidden. Can you do that?"

Ana nods, her eyes wide and scared, but she doesn't hesitate to take the infant.

I close the door behind them and hope they go

unnoticed, because shit's about to get real, and I'm just going out on a limb here, but I'm pretty sure it will not go well if all the dragons in the world discover we are trying to kidnap the only baby dragon in existence. I mean, I could be misreading the situation, but given the glares I'm getting from the Night brothers, I'm pretty sure I'm not.

"Why do my children fight amongst themselves?" the Mother of Dragons demands, her voice carrying over time and space and into the very souls of each of us, or so it feels.

Dath'Racul looks cowed—and I rather enjoy seeing the arrogant ass taken down a few notches by mommy. But then I look at the golden dragon again and feel my insides coil and wrap around themselves and my brief delight at his discomfort turns to reluctant empathy. This is not a woman to mess with.

"Mother," Racul says, his voice still powerful despite his humbled position. "Ventus attacked me, accusing me of taking the life of Lyx, but it is not true."

Amora seems to grow in size as her anger envelops her like a cloak. "Two of my children have died. Two immortal beings of ultimate power ripped from the worlds. It is unthinkable. Who has done this thing?" she demands. "It was not one of you, it cannot be one of you. That would be beyond blasphemous."

"I do not believe it was any of us," Racul says, tossing a cross look at his brother. "Ava'Kara gave her life voluntarily," he offers.

Amora scoffs. "I am well aware of what Kara did and why. To preserve this dilapidated, failed experiment of a world. As if the life and soul of a dragon was worth this scrap heap."

My blood boils at her words, and my spine stiffens as I listen. Derek shoots me a cautioning glance.

"What has become of Kara's child? Where is my grandchild?" Amora looks around as if one of the dragons might magically produce her from thin air.

I shift uncomfortably and pointedly do not look at the carriage, even though we might as well be invisible to the dragons. Which suits me just fine.

"We have not yet been to the scene of the crime," Racul admits. "We do not know where the child is."

"Because you were too busy fighting amongst yourselves," she shouts, her words like daggers piercing the hearts of her children. "Behaving much like the vagabond you created this world for."

They all drop their heads. It's clear there's no good answer to that, so they don't try.

"And what of Lyx'Ara?" Amora asks. "Her death was not voluntary. Someone must pay."

"We will begin an investigation," Racul says. "Her killer will suffer."

"You are correct in that my child," she says, a saccharine smile spreading over her lips but never reaching her hard golden eyes. "That is why I have come. To punish those who would harm my children."

Ventus'Arak, the Air Dragon, glances up. "What is your plan?" he asks cautiously.

"My plan," she says, stepping forward, "is to end this little experiment. Once you have found my grandchild and left this miserable excuse for a world, I will destroy it and all who still remain, including my daughter's murderer."

My heart drops to my gut, and even the dragons look shocked.

"Mother, please reconsider," Racul says. "This is our home."

She holds up her hand and a beam of golden light shoots from her palm, hitting Racul in the gut. He stumbles back, grunting in pain. "This is not your home, child. This is your creation, but it is not your home. Your home awaits you in our true world, unencumbered by the muddy mixed races of these substandard beings you've surrounded yourselves with. I've indulged you long enough, and this indulgence has cost me two of my children. I will allow it no longer."

"No!" I shout, stepping forward, the words rush out of my mouth before I can change my mind. I can feel the frustrated and frightened looks of the brothers on me as I approach closer to the dragon.

She turns her attention to me, and it is a fright to behold her direct gaze. "Who dares speak to me!" It's not a question, it's a command.

"Eve Oliver," I say as my power fills me, just as it did the night I confronted Cole. "The Maiden Fate returned." The past, present and future collide, and I feel myself rising from the ground, glowing with light, tinged by darkness, all the elements swirling around me. Wind whipping my hair. The earth cracking under me, bubbling with spurts of water. Fire lighting my finger tips.

I hear the gasps of the other dragons as they witness my transformation, but I keep my eyes locked on the Mother of Dragons. Though the Dragon Council might once have seemed intimidating, they pale in comparison to her formidable presence.

"A return of the Fates," she says, gliding towards me until we are face to face. "What intriguing timing. Tell me, do you know who took my daughter's life?"

"Not yet," I admit. "But give me time. I will find the truth. I will find justice for your daughter, who was also my friend. But you cannot destroy this world."

Lightning cracks around her and her eyes glow a violent gold as power surges around us. "You dare tell me what I can or cannot do, Fate?"

My power pulses and grows, enveloping us both. It's a pissing contest, but a necessary one. She will only respond to power. I feel this instinctively and know I cannot back down. "I do. This world does not belong to you. It no longer belongs to just the dragons. It is all of ours. And it is mine. My soul flows in the lakes and streams, my blood feeds the roots of the trees, my magic powers the winds and sparks the fires... this world is now a part of me, and I cannot let you destroy it."

Her eyes widen and her golden light pools out into long tendrils that extend from her body and dive into the ground, as if testing my claims. "It seems you are correct. You have become part of this world." She doesn't sound happy at the proclamation, but I press my advantage while I can.

"There are good people here. Innocent people. They do not deserve to die for the crime of one."

She pauses, considering her next words. "You may very well be one of the Fates returned, but you are weak without an Order. In the past, the Fates were aided by the Druids, who shared their power and strengthened them. What do you have? You have no sisters. You have no Order. You are nothing."

My power seems to dim at her words, and I don't know how to respond. I hadn't considered the position the Fates had in the past and how that might impact me in the present. It's been a lot to wrap my mind around as it is.

My thoughts race as I flash through everything I've read and learned trying to think of an adequate response, but nothing useful comes to mind. Then Sebastian steps forward, joining me, and bends down on one knee. "I am one of the original Druids and I pledge myself to Eve. She is not alone."

I look down at the handsome Earth Druid, overcome by emotion at his declaration. But before I can respond, Liam steps forward as well.

"I too pledge myself to the Maiden Fate. My power is hers. My service is hers. I am hers."

"And I," says Elijah, joining his brothers.

"We all pledge ourselves," says Derek, taking his place. All four of the brothers are kneeling at my feet, as Amora and I float above the ground in a cloud of power.

The golden dragon studies the Night brothers thoughtfully. "You were a powerful Order once," she says. "And I can see that your magic have returned. But I am surprised that after all that happened, you four would willingly commit yourself to the Fates once more, given all that entails."

I want to ask what 'all that entails' means, but this doesn't seem like a great time to interrupt.

"We commit ourselves to Eve," Sebastian says stubbornly.

"Very well," she says. "Formalize your vows and I will reconsider." She holds up a hand and produces a golden ceremonial dagger and matching bowl, and hands it to Elijah.

Amora moves away from us and the Night brothers circle me as I lower myself to the ground. Then they each call upon their element, letting it dance between us. Fire, earth, air, water.

I can't help but thinking we're missing the light and darkness Cole would bring. But I push aside that thought and focus.

Elijah slices his palm, causing the blood to pool on his skin, then lets the blood drop into the bowl before he passes both to Sebastian. Around the circle they go, cutting into their own flesh, letting it drop into the bowl.

Once all four have done so, Liam, the last to use the blade, reaches for my hand, and I offer it to him, letting him slice into my palm. My blood mixes with the brothers' and Liam takes the bowl and sips it, then passes it around. When it finally returns to me, I realize I'm meant to drink the blood that is left. So I do.

As soon as the mixture of our blood slides down my throat I see the bonds between us form, like silver chords attaching each of us, and I'm suddenly much more aware of them, their feelings, their presence, their magic. It's heady, to feel this deeply intimate connection.

"Very well," Amora says. "I will give you a fortnight to discover who killed my daughter and bring them to me. If you do not, I will destroy this world and you with it. If you do, I will spare this world."

Two weeks. That's not enough time, but it will have to do. "I will need the cooperation of the other dragons to accomplish this in such a short time. And I will need full authority to do whatever must be done."

"As you wish," she says, gesturing for the Dragon Council to approach. "You, my beloveds, are under the temporary authority of the Maiden Fate, who is tasked with finding my daughter's killer. Give her your rings, and afford her every liberty and cooperation. I expect you will not disappoint me in this," she says, giving each of them, as well as me, a pointed glare.

They look none too happy at this proclamation and grumble under their breaths, but they do not argue.

The Earth Dragon steps forward first, tugging the ring off her finger and handing it to me.

Each of them follow suit, silently relinquishing their authority to someone they clearly consider a lesser being. Or at least they did before they found out who I really am.

Still, dragons are not easily humbled. They will obey their mother, but they don't have to like it.

Once I've slipped all their rings onto my fingers, I pause, studying them, wondering what use they are, other than implied authority.

As if sensing my question, Amora shows me her ring. "These symbols on the sides of the ring, if you channel your magic and trace them into the air, will summon the dragon whose ring you are using."

Wow. This is better than text messaging, at least in terms of access. Though I don't particularly want to summon pissed off dragons to me at any given moment.

Racul's face is a study in frustrated anger. "Do not abuse this temporary privilege," he growls.

I smile charmingly at him. "My only goal is solving this murder and saving the world. I'm sure we both want the same thing in this, do we not?"

He glances away, unwilling to answer directly.

Amora begins to float upward, slowly shifting into

her dragon form. "I will have eyes on you all. Do not disappoint."

And then she flies through the tear in the sky and disappears.

I look to the dragons, a bit flabbergasted by the shift in power dynamic. But we don't have a lot of time, so I need to start getting answers.

"First question for all of you," I say, skipping the small talk. "What, besides another dragon, can kill one of you?"

Racul glances at her siblings and then scowls at me. "There is nothing else that can kill a dragon."

"So it was one of you," I challenge.

"No." His answer is curt.

"I'm sure you can see how this creates a problem. You do want to save the world don't you?"

From the corner of my eye, I see Callia appear, her silver eyes glowing like the horn on her head, her skin and hair as black as ink. The unicorn woman shifts to my side and whispers in my ear. "They are lying to you. There is one other thing that can kill a dragon." She turns to face me, the horn on her head glowing a bright —nearly blinding—silver. "Me."

THE VISION

The night is darkening round me,
The wild winds coldly blow ;
But a tyrant spell has bound me,
And I cannot, cannot go.
~Emily Bronte, The Night is Darkening
Around Me

THE DRAGONS each transform and fly away, leaving me stunned and deflated as my magic drains from me. Callia is still here, her eyes now locked on the tear in the sky the Mother of Dragons just disappeared into. I leave her to her thoughts and turn to the brothers, who stand beside me like sentinels.

"What the hell just happened?" I ask nobody in particular.

Elijah grins. "I think you just became the most powerful person in this world."

"Shit."

Sebastian runs a hand through his hair, a frown tugging at his lips. "This is... complicated. You bought us time, but if we don't solve this murder, she'll hold you personally responsible."

"I'm not sure how that's any worse than her destroying the world today with us in it," I point out as we walk back to the carriage.

"Good point," Sebastian says, though the worry has not left his face.

I look down at the rings lining my fingers. All six of the dragon rings plus Cole's ring. I can feel the power in them all zinging through my flesh, sending goose-bumps up my arms. "We need to get Ana and Zara home," I say. "And then we've got to get to work."

We also need to talk about the oaths they all just took, but right now isn't the time. First, I need to find out more from Callia about how she can kill dragons.

"Explain," I tell her, and the brothers glance at me, then realize I'm talking to an invisible unicorn and studiously ignore us.

"The only way to kill a dragon—other than being a dragon yourself—is to puncture their heart with a unicorn horn," she says.

She glances away, as if caught in a long-forgotten memory. "There were many of us once upon a time. We galloped over the lands free and wild. Until one day, a unicorn and a dragon got into an argument, and the unicorn ran the dragon through with his horn. The dragon died, shocking everyone. This was so long ago most on this world wouldn't remember it, but still the story spread, and then we were hunted, our horns fetching top price from illegal traders. The dragons, fearing the risk we posed, even those of us loyal to the Council, did the unspeakable. They quietly had all the unicorns killed and had all our horns destroyed by dragon fire."

"Did they kill you?" I ask, stunned by the cruelty of it all.

"Yes." But she doesn't expand as we reach the carriage.

I leave the questions for later as I examine the busted wheel. "Couldn't earth magic fix this?" I ask Sebastian.

"No, this is dead wood. I can't manipulate something that has no life left in it."

"You can," Callia whispers into my ear. "You have all the elements and can therefore sing to the parts that are dead, and the parts that yet live."

I'm used to these impromptu lessons from her, and I love stretching my powers, so I concentrate and focus on the wheel, on the molecules that form it, and I visualize it repairing itself like a broken bone. As I do, the wheel shifts, shakes, and begins to move together, the splintered pieces fusing back into one seamlessly, until it's entirely restored.

"Is there any limit to your power?" Sebastian asks, in awe.

"I don't know. How would I fare in a straight up fight with the Mother of Dragons?" I ask. "Because if we don't do what she wants, it might come to that."

They all look like they're about to shit themselves at the suggestion. Even Callia shakes her head.

"You are not ready to face her," Callia says. "She's much more powerful than you can possibly imagine."

I detect equal measure awe and fear in her voice, and I wonder how well she knows the golden dragon. I'm still not entirely used to dealing with beings who have lived such ancient lives. It's a perspective that's hard to fit into a human-sized lifespan.

"You cannot fight her," Elijah says, speaking over Callia.

"Yeah, I just got the lecture from the unicorn. I get it. Let's do our jobs so I don't have to." I reach for the carriage to get in, when Callia passes a hand over mine and a flash grips me so hard my stomach clenches and I double over in pain, vomiting what little food is in my stomach.

Liam rushes to my side, holding my hips as I continue to heave.

He's speaking, but I can't hear him, as my head pounds with the grip of a vision I can't stop or control.

Callia stands before me, but she looks different. Her horn is missing, shaved off at the base. And then the vision shifts and I see a rider on horseback, making a mad dash through the woods towards the portal. He wears a black cloak and at his hip is a dagger that glows silver, made from unicorn horn.

And he's trying to leave the Otherworld. Ahead of him the Dragon's Breath wall looms large, and he's heading straight towards it.

The vision begins to fade, and through the pounding in my head, I force it to last just a little longer. I need to get a closer look. To see who's on the horse.

Something burns my eyes and just before I slam back into my own body, I see his face.

No.

It can't be.

Pain grips me as Liam continues to hold me, his body hot against mine.

I realize I'm crying and swipe at my eyes, only to find crimson staining my hand. Was I crying blood?

"Eve!" Liam's voice finally penetrates my haze and I feel power from all four brothers pour into me, relieving the pain in my head and in my gut.

I struggle to sit up and find that the world is spinning just a little bit less. "I'm okay," I say.

I look around for the unicorn and find her standing to the side, her face unreadable. "What was that?" I ask her.

"I am still connected to my horn," she says. "And you just saw a vision of where it is right now."

I stand and Liam offers support, but I feel stronger and stronger by the moment. "I have to go," I say.

"We're going home," Liam insists.

"No, you all get the kids home. I have a lead on a possible murder weapon. I'll explain later but I don't have time now."

I look too Callia for guidance. "How do I get there?" I ask her.

She shrugs. "You could always try flying."

My eyes widen in stunned amazement. "Fly? I can fly?"

"Well, you have hovered before," Elijah says. "That's not how air magic is supposed to work but..."

"That's not how *his* air magic works," Callia says. "But you're different. Don't let them limit you. Try it. It's the only way you'll make it there before the suspect gets away."

I nod and focus, calling on my air and light magic. And just like that, I am airborne. I look down at the Night brothers. "I'll meet you back at the castle. Trust me."

I know they'll just argue with me, so I don't wait for their response. I take off flying high and fast, manipulating the winds around my body to give me speed without discomfort. I use my fire magic to warm me and earth magic to stabilize me. For a moment I forget what I saw in the vision. I forget about Lyx dying. About the orphaned children we are bringing home. And I am completely absorbed in the present moment, relishing the freedom and intoxicating wonder of doing something that previously I'd only done in dreams.

I truly can't believe I'm actually flying. Racing through the air like a bird, wind and freedom all around me.

But the flight ends too soon, as I reach the edge of the world, the grove where Kaya's tree lives, and the place where the rider was headed.

I see him now. He's moments from reaching the portal.

I drop down from the sky and land right in front of him. He swerves his horse to avoid knocking me over, and then topples off gracelessly.

He storms over to me, his face a confusing play of emotions when he sees me.

"Eve?"

"Hello, Cole."

There's a lump in my throat as I say his name. The last time we saw each other, I found out he'd been lying to me about everything, and he discovered I was the Fate who ordered his torture. Being this close to him now is almost painful. All the hurt and anger are there, but so is the love, the desire, the passion he ignited in me. He feels achingly familiar and like a stranger all at once. I want to reach out and touch him, to pull him into me, to feel his lips on mine, but he's standing here, trying to flee the Otherworld, with a weapon that could kill a dragon hanging from his hip.

"What are you doing here?" he asks.

"I was just going to ask the same of you."

He shakes his head, clearly confused. "I'm riding a horse."

"Obviously. I mean where are you going?"

He shrugs. "I'm enjoying the afternoon before a meeting I have scheduled."

"A meeting?" I scoff at that. "Does your meeting involve killing dragons?" I ask. Though I sound flippant, my heart is racing in my chest and I feel close to vomiting again. I can't bear for him to be guilty of this crime, but I can't ignore who he is, or what he is capable of.

"What are you talking about?" he asks.

"Lyx. She's dead. Stabbed through the heart with something that looks suspiciously like that unicorn horn dagger you've got there."

His face pales and he stumbles back a bit. "Lyx is dead? Are you sure?"

"I saw her body myself."

His eyes widen. "Her body remains? How? Why?"

"That's what I'm trying to figure out, Cole," I say with as much cool as I can muster. "The Mother of Dragons herself showed up and is pretty pissed. Things will not end well for me if I don't solve this murder, and right now, you look like the prime suspect."

"*Mon Couer*, I didn't do this. You must believe me. Look at your ring if you think I am lying." He glances down at my hand and raises an eyebrow when he sees all the dragon rings lining my fingers.

I don't even bother considering his suggestion. "Do you really think I still believe this ring protects me from your lies?" I ask. "I've known for some time that it's a tracking device more than anything."

He cocks his head, his dark eyes unreadable. "You are a surprising woman. If you know, then why do you still wear it?" he asks, stepping closer to me until we are inches apart from each other. He raises a hand to caress my cheek, and though a part of me wants to turn away, I find I cannot. I'm mesmerized by him, as I always have been, and despite everything, I still crave him, body, mind and soul, and the bastard knows it.

I force myself to step back, just out of his reach, though the action pains me. "I wear it as a reminder not to fall for a pretty face."

He grins, stroking his chin. "I am rather dashing, it's true."

I roll my eyes but can't help but laugh. "You're impossible is what you are."

"By the looks of it, you're quite skilled at handling the impossible, *mon cher.*"

"I'm not here to flirt with you," I say, though my voice lacks the confidence I try desperately to instill in it.

"Of course not. How can I be of service? If you do not believe me, how shall I prove my innocence to you?"

"Where did you get the dagger?" I ask. "And where are you going with it?"

"It was not easy to track down," he says. "When the Collector went missing, he left a certain gap in the underground industry. I, in my benevolence, have volunteered to fill that gap by acquiring that which is hard to find for people with the right resources."

My face hardens. "I hope you haven't picked up all his criminal behavior," I say, thinking of the girls he trafficked in.

Cole frowns. "No. Never. You know me better than that. I would never trade in lives. Not for any amount of money. Only hard to come by goods."

I nod, believing him this time. I know his past, know what he's been through, and I know he wouldn't put someone else through that.

He cocks his head, studying me. "You wouldn't happen to know what became of the Collector, would you?" he asks.

I shrug. "Why would I know anything about that?" I say. I mean, it's not exactly a lie. Just a question.

He chuckles. "Of course. How silly of me."

"So you were hired to find this dagger," I say, bringing us back to the point of the conversation.

"Yes," he says. "But I'm under strict orders of confidentiality."

I cock my hip and stare him down. "Cole."

He glances down at my hands again, at the rings lining them. "*Merdre,*" he says, cursing under his breath. "I literally can't tell you. I'm bound. But there's nothing saying I can't show you. Come with me to my meeting."

"Yes. I will. But how is that better for you than telling me?"

He shrugs. "It's a loophole. And I get to spend more time with you this way. That constitutes a win-win in my mind."

"Fine. Take me to your meeting." I studiously ignore the flare of joy I feel at knowing we will have more time together. "But before you do, you should put a tracker on that dagger so we can see what happens to it."

"I could," he says. "But it would be better if you did it yourself. I can teach you how."

What is it with everyone wanting to teach me new tricks like I'm a dog to be trained? I sigh, but at the same time, this knowledge will come in handy. My powers are growing with each passing day, and though I keep waiting to hit the limits of what I can do, it hasn't happened yet.

"Fine," I say, begrudgingly.

Cole smiles and approaches me. He pulls out the dagger and places it in my hand, then stands behind me, his arms circling my shoulders.

I suck in a breath at his closeness, as I feel the dark tendrils of his magic interlace with mine so naturally, so organically, in such a way that I couldn't stop it even if I wanted to.

And I don't want to.

I want to stay here forever. I want to bring him home with me. I want him to be a part of my family.

But I can't always have what I want.

So instead I focus on the magic.

He recites ancient words in my ear, his breath sending shivers up my spine, and I repeat the spell and channel the darkness inside of me, as I feel him do.

The power is excited to be let out as Cole shifts closer to me. "Your darkness is tired of being stifled, *mon couer*. You must let it out lest it eat you from the inside."

"That's a charming imagery," I say. "Thanks."

The dagger in my hand becomes shrouded in dark mist, then settles into its normal self once more. "Did it work?"

Cole nods. "When you want to know where it is, repeat the words I taught you."

I hand it to him and do as instructed, and when I close my eyes, I see the dagger in his hand, clear as day. Then the vision pans out so I see both of us, where we are, what we are doing. It's a bit disconcerting seeing myself as a third person in my mind's eye, but it's a useful trick.

I open my eyes again and nod. "It worked."

He grins. "You're a natural."

He holds out his hand then, and I reluctantly take it, relishing the cool comfort he offers. "Ready for our meeting?" he asks.

I nod.

"Do you trust me?"

I don't know how to answer that, so I say nothing.

He sighs. "Just hold onto me once we enter the portal. It's going to be a wild ride."

Merdre. It's my turn to swear under my breath. Because in this, Cole Night is not lying.

THE DAGGER

Perhaps if Death is kind, and there can be returning,
  We will come back to earth some fragrant night,
  ~Sara Teasdale, If Death is Kind

IT IS INDEED A WILD RIDE, one that, had I anything left in my stomach, would have resulted in said content being spewed all over Cole's sexy black cloak. But, as it is, that gift was already betowed somewhere in the forests of the new world.

Entering the portal is easy enough—it's like sliding through warm butter. It's when he dematerializes us into black mist that things go from manageable to what the actual hell.

I feel as if I'm being turned inside out and shredded into tiny pieces, then blown apart like some kind of macabre wishing flower.

I exist in nothingness. It's not black, or dark, it's just nothing. Cole's voice reverberates around me, coming from all directions and no direction at all at the same time. "Embrace your darkness, Eve."

I swear to all the gods if I get one more bumper sticker motivational talk from him, Callia, or any of the other Night brothers I might scream.

Hell, I might be screaming at this very moment. Since I feel as if I've ceased to exist, it's hard to tell.

When we finally materialize, I hit the ground hard, knocking the wind out of my lungs, despite my budding mastery of my air magic.

"Was that absolutely necessary?" I ask Cole once I can speak again.

He is standing over me looking as if he just had a leisurely stroll through the Garden of Eden and not a hellscape ride through the Underworld.

"How else would you propose we get here?" he asks, gesturing around us.

For the first time, I take note of where we are. And how freaking cold it is. I tap into my fire magic to warm myself up, now that physical sensations are returning, and I turned slowly to look around. To the west of us is a vast expanse of pristine topiary gardens, featuring mythical creatures of all kinds carved from bushes the color of eggplants, dotted with pure white flowers that form their own designs. Everything covered in a thin layer of fluffy white snow, though the sky is clear and sunny at present. To the east of us is nothing but sky. We landed dangerously close to the edge of the world, or so it would seem. We are surrounded by clouds, and it's impossible to tell how far up we are.

In the distance is a castle that looks made of crystal, glistening in the sun.

The sun! I look up and see it peeking through the clouds and close my eyes, enjoying the warmth against my face for a brief moment before I remember why we are here.

"We are back on earth?" I ask.

"We are, though you will not find this place on any maps. It exists in a hidden realm—a floating island that belongs to my client."

"The client you still can't tell me the name of," I say.

"Correct."

He holds his arm out to me in a gentlemanly fashion. "Shall we, *mon coeur?*"

Every time he calls me one of his terms of endearment, I melt a little inside, but I must be careful with him. So I ignore his offer of an escort and begin walking to the castle on my own. He dashes to catch up with me, the cheeky grin he wears never slipping from his face.

"I see we are still on the outs?" he asks, keeping pace with me as we weave through the garden.

"Cole," I say as steadily as I can. "You pretended to be my dead twin and confessed to a heinous crime, all in your efforts to hurt your brothers. Then you disappeared. So yeah, we're a bit on the outs."

For the first time, his grin slips and a look of serious contemplation replaces it on his devilishly handsome face. "I didn't think about what my pain would cost you," he says softly, and my heart cracks a little at his vulnerability. "When we are broken, we tend to break others until we mend our own brokenness."

"And are you mending yours?" I ask.

He stops walking to face me, taking my hand in his and running a finger over his ring. "I am trying my very best. When the cracks in your soul run this deep for this long, it is not an easy process to heal. But I will do anything to repair what I have broken between us."

"Swear to me you didn't have anything to do with Lyx's murder," I say.

"I swear it to you," he says. "I want to catch her killer as badly as you do. She was my mentor, and my friend. Her death is a great loss to all."

"Then let's solve this murder and see where things lead between us. And between your brothers."

He squeezes my hand, and he doesn't let go as we continue walking. This time I don't pull away as I tell him about my training, about Callia, and about my confrontation with the Mother of Dragons. "And you should know, the Order of Druids has reformed," I say. "Your brothers swore oaths to me, though I'm not entirely sure what it all means."

He stiffens and glances at me curiously. "That is

significant. But if anyone is worthy of that power, it is you."

I wonder what is going through his mind at this news. The Order did not treat him well, to say the least, particularly the Maiden Fate, my past self, who destroyed his life. But that was such a long time ago and so much has changed. I may be the Maiden Fate reincarnated, but I'm also still me. I will not become lost in who she was, which, by all accounts, wasn't always good. I will temper her influence with my own sense of right and wrong. Hopefully that will be enough.

We arrive at the castle a solid hour later, and I'm slightly out of breath from the altitude.

"Use your air magic," Cole says as the door opens of its own accord. "You have no idea yet how powerful you are."

"Yeah, so I'm told," I say as I manipulate the air currents around me to ease my breathing.

A man in a butler's uniform answers the door and without a word ushers us in, though he casts glances at me curiously. "He is expecting you," he tells Cole.

We follow him up a winding stone staircase to the very top of the castle, and as we step out we are greeted by Cole's client.

"Ventus'Arak, the Air Dragon, is your client?" I whisper, as the dragon shifts from his true form to his human form.

"Why have you brought the Fate with you?" he demands of Cole.

"Is there a reason you don't want me to know you've gone to great lengths to acquire the only weapon that can kill a dragon?" I ask, holding up my fingers full of dragon rings to remind him his own damn mother sent me on this mission.

Cole raises an eyebrow and looks amused at the exchange, though he says nothing.

"I will know if it is the weapon that took my sister's life," Ventus says as he stalks over to us, his pale blue eyes narrowed to a slit.

The Air Dragon is tall, at least a head taller than Cole, which is saying something, with broad shoulders that taper to a perfectly toned six pack. I know this because his entire outfit consists of his iridescent blue wings that drape like a cloak, and what can only be described as a loin cloth. There isn't much left to the imagination, and even though the sight is impressive, I need to stay focused on something other than his abs.

"How can you be so sure?" I ask.

He holds his hand out. "The dagger, please?"

"Payment?" Cole asks, pulling the weapon from the leather sheath at his hip.

Ventus huffs as if he's been personally offended, but he grabs a leather coin purse from a wooden table nearby and tosses it to Cole, who catches it with one hand while handing off the unicorn dagger with the other.

Ventus studies it, waving a hand over it until it glows. And like Memory Catchers, the dagger projects holographic-like images of various beings dying at the end of the blade. There aren't many, but watching it feels awful, like some kind of medieval snuff film. When the images fade, I realize what he means.

"It holds the memory of all the lives it has taken," I say. "And Lyx isn't there."

Ventus nods, then turns to Cole. "Where did you find it?" he asks.

Cole glances at me before he answers. "In the private quarters of Dath'Racul."

Ventus looks confused for a moment. "This is the last of its kind that remains in our world. I suspected Racul of killing our sister, but he wouldn't need the dagger to do that."

"Do you really think he's guilty?" I ask. That would make this mystery easy to solve... if I could find proof.

He looks away from us, over the ledge of his castle into the distance. "I reacted impetuously upon her death," he says softly. "She and I were always close, even after she left the Council. I understood her in ways the others didn't, and she was a trusted confidant. I confess I lost a part of myself when I felt her die. But I no longer believe he killed her. Taking the life of another dragon would go against everything we are. Even Racul is not that ruthless."

He studies the dagger in his hand, running the pad of his finger along the razor edge. "Perhaps it is time for the Age of Dragons to come to an end. We began this world with noble intentions, but power and greed have corrupted even the best of us."

A strong wind blows through as he speaks, carrying the scent of snow about to fall as Ventus walks to the edge of the roof, his toes hanging off the ledge.

It's a long fall off the top of a castle this height, but I remind myself he's a dragon. Fear of heights is probably not one of his problems.

"We lost our way long ago," he says. "But we truly paved the path to our descent into darkness when we slaughtered the unicorns in an effort to preserve our own immortality. It's unnatural for any race to be so powerful that none can defeat it. The unicorns were our balance, and we killed them all out of fear."

Cole's eyes widen at that, and I'm surprised he's admitting this when none of them would speak about it earlier. Even with their mother's orders hanging over them, they hadn't wanted to admit that a unicorn horn could kill them. Something about the Air Dragon seems different this time. More melancholy and reflective.

"Do you know who might have killed Lyx?" I ask, hoping against all odds this whole trip hasn't been a dead end.

He turns to look at me, his eyes unreadable. "You should ask my mother," he says. "She carries within her secrets that could destroy worlds."

My ears perk at that, and I make a mental note to find out more.

He studies the dagger again. "It is time to step aside and let the world move on without me," he says, and before I can comprehend what's happening, Ventus thrusts the blade into his own heart.

I scream and Cole wraps his arm around my waist to keep me from rushing towards the dying dragon.

He smiles briefly, holding the dagger until his body disintegrates into a pale blue dust and is carried away on the wind, the blade dropping to the ground with a thud.

It shimmers briefly and projects a final image of Ventus dying, a new memory for its collection, before returning to normal.

Cole lets me go and I rush to the edge, looking over as if I might see the dragon reappear like this was a cruel and elaborate prank. But he doesn't. He's gone. Another dragon has died.

That's three since I arrived in this world.

A world that hasn't seen a dragon die for as long as the Night brothers have been alive.

What have I brought with me to cause this destruction, I wonder, as Cole pulls me into an embrace and the tears I've been holding back flow freely.

THE SWIM

The fountains mingle with the river
  And the rivers with the ocean,
  The winds of heaven mix for ever
  With a sweet emotion;
  Nothing in the world is single;
  All things by a law divine
  In one spirit meet and mingle.
  Why not I with thine?—
  ~Percy Bysshe Shelley, Love's Philosophy

THE BUTLER INTERRUPTS US, his face grim as he studies the scene. "You both should leave. The dragons will know of his death and come to investigate. It would be better for all if you were not found here."

"How will you explain what happened?" I ask.

"I will not have to," he says, and holds up a Memory Catcher. "My master left a message for his siblings, but it is private."

I look to Cole, who nods, and I realize we will have to dematerialize to get out of here quickly. The dagger is still laying on the floor where the dragon dropped it, and with a flick of my wrist I use air magic to fly it to my waiting hand, then tuck it into my waistband. Cole is the only one who sees, and he raises an eyebrow with a grin like he's proud of me. Then he pulls me against his chest.

"Ready, *mon coeur*?"

"No," I say.

"Just relax," he whispers, as his hands rest on my hips. "Use your darkness."

I swallow and nod, then reluctantly tug on the powers deep within me, the dark depth I'm most scared of tapping into, and I let it flow into me, and then through me.

"Very good," Cole says. "Now stretch your darkness into me and feel what I do. You can do this without me, you just have to align yourself to the frequency of this spell, in a manner of speaking. And then picture where you want to go with as much detail as you can."

Per his instruction, I stretch the tendrils of darkness flowing out of me and attach to him, our magic merging, pulsing as one. The feeling is nearly erotic and brings to mind our love making, when our bodies were so connected they felt as one.

I can feel from the shift in his pants that he's thinking the same thing, and that only makes my own arousal more powerful.

He pulls me even tighter toward him until my breasts are pressed against his rock hard chest. My breath hitches as our bodies connect. And then we are traveling, our physical selves unraveling within the nothingness that consumes us.

But this time, I do not feel the panic and pain as before. Instead, I feel as if my spirit is set free, and I am everything, and nothing.

After an indefinite amount of time, that could have been mere seconds or centuries, we arrive within the portal and are pushed through into the Otherworld, bodies intact, souls contained within our dense meat forms.

For a moment I feel encumbered by the weight of my flesh, and I briefly mourn the feeling I had when we traveled through nothing.

Cole is still holding tight to me, his lips inches from mine. "You catch on fast," he whispers, his dark eyes luminous and intoxicating.

Still caught up in the swirl of emotions, I can't stop myself from pulling his head down and pressing my lips to his. I've dreamed of tasting his mouth again, of feeling his tongue flick over my lips, of reveling in the delight and desire that he brings.

He moans against my mouth, his chest rumbling with untapped longing, and I press my hips against him. He hardens against my stomach and I slide my hand down his chest until I'm caressing him.

He nibbles at my lip, then traces kisses down my neck to my collar bone, his teeth grazing me, nipping at my skin. My other hand is wrapped around his back, nails digging into him. I want more than I can have right now, and the thought sobers me. I gently pull away, my lips swollen with his kisses, my body empty without him.

"I should go," I say, reluctantly. "This is too soon."

He caresses my head and nods. "*Je comprends*. But I am not giving up on us. I hope you do not either."

Tears sting my eyes as he steps back and disappears into smoke.

I look around at the forest, alive with the sounds of the wild, as I wipe my eyes and straighten my back.

Someday I might get him back, but today is not that day, and I need to go home. The others are probably losing their damn minds right now.

I contemplate the easiest way to go back to the castle. I could fly, but that will take a decent amount of time.

Or I could try my new shadow powers. That would get me home in an instant, but it also low key terrifies me.

I opt for being terrified. Because if I can master this, it's a useful trick to have in my tool box.

I close my eyes and pull out my darkness while

reminding myself what his magic felt like when he did this. Then I imagine the gardens just outside the castle, where I first found Moon.

It seems to be the safest place to aim for, and the one which will likely be the most discreet as well, since no one has seen me do this and it might freak them out a bit if I appear before them randomly.

Just as before, I disintegrate into nothing, into shadow and darkness, and then arrive just where I intended. Well, mostly where I intended. Since I was thinking of Moon and how I found him, I actually find myself stuck in the damn bush that he was stuck in when I rescued him. And it hurts like a bitch.

I slowly tear myself out of the dangerous barbed bushes and I'm covered in scratches that are starting to bleed.

That's how Liam finds me.

"What happened?" he asks, running over to me, his eyes filled with worry. "Who attacked you?"

He takes my arms and studies the injuries as I point to the offending bush. "We had a bit of a misunderstanding," I explain.

"I'm sure there's a story in that somewhere, but come in and let's get you cleaned up. Everyone is worried sick about you. Where did you go?"

"I'll explain once we're all together."

Liam slips an arm around me and we walk into the castle, then he leaves to round everyone up and find some ointment for my cuts. Moon greets me in the hall and rubs up against my legs purring aggressively. I pick him up and nuzzle his soft black fur to my face. "I've missed you," I whisper, and I swear he purrs even louder. I set him down and he follows me as I head to the library.

The great hearth is stoked with a blazing fire and Alina and the baby dragon, Zara—who's presently in her human form—are both in the crib together. They are playing with colorful blocks of wood. Alina lights them on fire and Zara giggles and spits water onto them to put the fire out. Then they both laugh and do it all over again.

Liam arrives with the ointment and smiles when he sees the babies. "They've been like that since the moment they met," he says.

"It looks like the fire proofing has worked," I note. We've been trying a lot of spells over the last several weeks to keep Alina from burning down everything she touches, and nothing has worked until now.

He nods. "I think adding the phoenix feather to the spell really helped," he says. "Good call."

I grin at the compliment as he begins applying the ointment to my skin.

It burns a bit, then creates a cooling sensation that sucks the pain away. By the time he's done, I feel as good as new, and I know my skin will heal in no time. Magic medicine is the best.

Sebastian arrives next and pulls me into a bear hug

that heals a much deeper part of my soul. Everything about this man makes me feel safe and cared for, and yet there is still a wall between us I don't know how to break down. But I'm determined to. Something always seems to get in the way of us being together more... intimately. That's going to end. Soon. I need this man. All of him.

As if sensing the direction of my thoughts, he tilts my head up and looks down at me, his forest green eyes full of so much unspoken longing.

"We should talk soon," I say softly. "Privately."

His pupils dilate and I feel how ready he instantly is for our 'talk.' "Just name the time and place, and I'm there."

But of course we are interrupted again when Elijah and Derek join us.

"Are Matilda and Lily coming?" I ask.

"Matilda is getting Ana to bed," Derek says. "And Lily is out with Kaya still."

"They haven't come back yet?" I ask, surprised. I know Lily went off to find the coroners, but I assumed she'd be home by now. Then again, Lily is home a lot less since she started dating Kaya, and I don't blame her. Being in a forest with her lover is likely far more exciting than being in a stuffy old castle.

"I'm sure she'll be back soon," Derek says. "Now please, share with us where you went. And how you suddenly learned to fly."

Oh right. Forgot about that.

That says something right there about how much has happened today, that learning to fly doesn't even register as worthwhile mentioning.

We take seats around the fire while the babies continue to play with their magic. Elijah brings me a glass of wine and he and Sebastian claim the spots to either side of me.

"Before I begin, I need you to all promise to zip your lips until I'm done. No matter what. Got it?" I glare at them each sternly until they all reluctantly agree.

And so I begin with the vision I saw of Cole in possession of a unicorn dagger heading out of the Otherworld.

"That puss-filled rodent," Sebastian seethes, and I shush him with a pinch to his arm.

"I said zip your lips."

He glowers but stays silent as I continue.

I finish my wine just as I finish my story, and Derek rises to refill my glass before pacing in front of the fire.

"The situation is escalating," Derek says. "We need to consider all our options. Having Ana and Zara here could backfire spectacularly."

"And where do you propose we send them?" I ask.

He glances away, because there's no good answer to that. "Anywhere that does not put you at risk and compromise our investigation."

"Ana is a potential witness," I say, "if you want to be

so bloody pragmatic about it. And Zara is a potential victim in need of protecting. Since we don't know who to trust outside this room, that leaves few options."

Derek, who is usually the even tempered one, snaps. "Damnit, Eve. You're thinking with your heart and not your head in this one!"

I stand, tired of this discussion. "Maybe this world needs more damn heart. It seems too many of you immortals get far too callous as the years tear out your emotions in favor of greed and self-serving nepotism."

And with that I storm out, too worn down to fight anymore.

Once in my room, the weight of the day adds a decade to how I feel, and I slough off my clothes and sink into the hot bath that's already waiting for me complete with scented oils. "Mable, did you do this?"

I look around for any sign of the ghost that looks after this castle and see my towel float to the edge of the bath.

I smile. "Thank you. It's much appreciated."

Moon takes his spot at the foot of my tub and proceeds to dip his paws into the water, splashing at things only he can see. I ignore him and close my eyes, content to let the heat soak out the exhaustion I feel.

I'm one giant prune and my limbs feel like noodles by the time I crawl out of the bathtub and dry myself, then slip into a silk robe and head to my room.

The sexy Fire Druid is sitting at the foot of my bed

with a vial of liquid in one hand and a jar of ointment in the other.

"This," he says, holding up the ointment, "is for the rest of those cuts."

I glance down at where he's looking and see my legs are pretty scratched up.

"And this," he says, indicating the vial, "is for the headache you have."

I raise an eyebrow. My head started pounding while I was in the bath. But... "how did you know?"

"It's a natural byproduct of pushing yourself too hard. You used some really advanced magic today and didn't give yourself time to recharge. There's going to be consequences."

I take the vial and down it in one gulp, cringing at the fowl taste. "Why do these always taste like ass? Can't you make something that tastes like strawberries?"

"Sure, I can, but it won't be medicinal. It's the rule. The worst it tastes, the better it works," he says with a wink.

"That's a terrible rule. By the power vested in me by the Mother of Dragons, I petition a change to this rule."

Liam laughs and pats the bed. "Settle in and I'll rub the ointment on you if you'd like."

By the gods I would like nothing more than to feel his hands all over my body, though I'm still too bloody pissed at Derek.

Still, I nod and let my robe fall to my feet. He studies my body with clear desire, but doesn't move until I'm lying on my stomach, eyes closed. Then he proceeds to massage out all the cuts and bruises, as well as the sore muscles that a day of intense—everything—has left. By the time he's done, I feel more relaxed.

"Thank you," I say, turning over to look at him. "I needed that."

He nods and heads to the door, then pauses. "I know we are all a pain in the ass at times. But know that Derek is just trying to protect you. We all are."

I sigh. "I know. But I'm not a broken little girl in need of protecting. Ana is though."

"I think Derek knows that. It's a complicated situation and he feels lost. He's used to being in charge of things, and he doesn't feel in charge of this. It scares him."

Damnit, I wanted to stay angry longer, but his words are softening my resolve.

"He's at the lake," Liam says. "In case that matters. He feels badly about the fight."

Well, shit.

Liam closes the door softly behind him and I sit in my bed stewing and trying to decide if I should go to the Water Druid or try to fall asleep, but thanks to Liam's words, sleep seems impossible now.

"Damn them both," I say as I climb out of my comfortable bed and aggressively put my robe on.

I make my way to my balcony and sigh. I guess I'm doing this.

Using my magic, I fly towards the lake just over the rise of trees to the north. It's part of our property, so it doesn't take too long, and I land at the edge of a large body of water, the Dragon's Breath shimmering off the glassy surface, making it look like a different kind of portal.

It's surrounded by trees and in the stillness of the evening it feels like the middle of nowhere.

Derek's clothes are folded neatly into a pile on a rock, and he is swimming laps in the water. When he turns to swim towards the shore, he sees me and stops. "Eve, what are you doing here?"

"Liam told me you were out here," I say. "I... I'm not sure why I came. I just don't like fighting with you."

"I don't like it either. Join me for a swim?"

I hesitate, but it's been so long since I've swam, and the night is perfect, and why the hell not? I let my robe fall to the ground and step into the lake, Derek's gaze unwavering from my body.

The water is cold and refreshing, and I don't cheat and use my fire magic to warm it. Instead, I let my body adjust to the temperature until I am submerged. Then I dunk under and swim towards Derek, popping up just in front of him.

"I'm sorry I lost my temper," he says softly, his wet dark hair gleaming under the Dragon's Breath. "I'm still conflicted about how I feel. Protecting you and our

family is my top priority, so it's difficult making decisions that go against that."

"I know," I say. "But we have to expand who we
think of as worthy of our protection," I say. "Especially
when it comes to children. Those kids need us."

He raises his hand to caress my face, moving closer
to me in the process.

My breasts graze his chest under water, and my
body responds instantly.

"You're the kindest soul I know," he says, and then
his lips are on mine and all I can think about is him.
Us. Our watery world where nothing else exists.

He was the first to offer me the job that changed
my life.

He defended me when his brothers didn't want me
in this world.

He brought me back to life.

And as his arm slips around my waist and I wrap
my legs around his, I feel us both coming to life once
again.

He tastes of the sea, or sunshine and rain and
sunsets on the beach. His lean, muscular body easily
supports us both and I feel how urgently he wants me
as he presses against my spread legs.

His hands slip down to my ass, his fingers digging
into my flesh as he tightens his hold on me, and our
magic blends, water splashing against water, as playful
as dolphins at sea.

Our kisses deepen, his teeth tugging at my lower

lip, then diving down, exploring my throat as I lean back.

I use our joined magic to push us up to the surface of the water, making a kind of waterbed for us that we spread out on, my body pinned beneath his.

Enjoying the access this position gives him to the rest of me, he teases and tastes every part of me, using his magic in thrilling new ways to take me to the edge.

We are cushioned by the element we both love, supported in this lake like a dream come to life, and when pleasure crashes into me in waves of nirvana, he does as well, filling me and driving me to new heights.

As he reaches his own climax, I join him again, and the bed beneath us pulls us under, letting us sink to the bottom of the lake, locked in our embrace. I use air magic to create a buffer around us and light magic to illuminate the underwater world we find ourselves in, as exotic fish swim past us and coral colored plant life sways in the currents.

He holds me tightly and I tuck myself into his arms, enjoying this unusual and magical moment for as long as I can.

Later, when our energy returns, we make our way to shore and dress.

Then we walk back to the castle together, hand in hand, enjoying the quiet moments of the evening, and when we reach my room, he hesitates, but I hold open the door. "Stay?"

He does.

That night I don't dream, but I do feel a deep warmth and safety as I drift on the clouds of my subconscious, and when I wake in the morning, Derek is still there, still holding me, his presence eternal and his love unshakable. He pulls me closer against him, his body wrapped around mine, my back pressed against his chest, and I feel his arousal as he drops kisses onto my neck.

I moan and press into him. "How long have you been awake?"

"Not too long."

I don't believe him, but it doesn't matter. I'm glad he stayed.

I press my ass against him, and he growls under his breath. "Don't you have to go to see Ifi and Elal soon?" he asks, his voice heavy with longing.

"Yes. So, we can't do a three hour marathon, but surely we have time for something?"

In a flash, Derek flips me over and pins me to the bed, pressing the weight of his body between my legs. "I can definitely give you something," he says as he trails kisses down my neck and to my breasts, stopping to give each their share of attention before moving further south. His fingers dig into my hips as he uses his tongue to push me to the edge of the cliff.

And then I'm falling. Pleasure crashes through me as he continues his attentions with his fingers, while positioning himself to plunge into me.

I bite his shoulder to keep from screaming in

ecstasy as he fills me, while he uses his hands to tease and torture other parts of me.

Once he climaxes, I'm ready again, and together we drown in each other's arms.

THE WEAPON

I am so small I can barely be seen.
How can this great love be inside me?
Look at your eyes. They are small,
But they see enormous things.
~Rumi, The Turn

AFTER THAT WAKE-UP WITH DEREK, I'm ready to have a productive day. I try not to let the weight of the world—literally—derail me from finding joy in the moment-to-moment blessings. So while I will do everything in my power to stop the destruction of the Otherworld—obviously—I also can't ignore the love and beauty I have around me every day. If anything, knowing how easily something can be torn from us, seeing the immortal greatness of dragons die, it has reminded me to stay present and be grateful for every moment I have with the ones I love.

I find Sebastian in the library, sitting by the fire and reading an old leather-bound book to Ana—who looks like a whole new child now that she's been bathed and dressed in clean clothes which fit her properly. Her golden hair shimmers against the fire light. Her cream skin is nearly translucent. And her eyes, a silvery blue, seem to shine when she looks at Sebastian.

He doesn't notice me yet and continues to read from the book, which is red with a silver title that reads, "All the Fairies Dared to Do."

"Platious never felt that she was brave or strong or right or good, and her name spoken aloud made her want to cover her ears," Sebastian says, pointing to a picture on the page. "Her wings sagged, and her hair never stayed where it was meant to, and her skin did not sparkle like the other fairies of the garden. So she felt herself plain. She did not yet know that within her held the seed of truth, and once planted, it would give her wisdom beyond measure."

Ana sees me and smiles, leaving Sebastian and running over to me for a hug.

"Hey, honey. Did you sleep well?"

She nods. "It was the most comfortable bed I've ever felt. Even my friend liked it."

"Your friend?"

Sebastian nods. "Every child needs an imaginary friend," he assures me with a wink.

"Of course," I say, smiling. "I'm glad you and your friend were comfortable." I put an arm over her shoulder and walk back to Sebastian. "Sounds like you were getting a fun story."

"Oh yes. I love Platious. She thinks she's not good, but she's *so* good. She just doesn't see it yet."

I share a glance with Sebastian, and I can tell we are both thinking about Cole. "Sometimes people need to be reminded of who they truly are before they can see the truth in themselves."

She nods sagely, then takes the book from Sebastian. "Can I keep reading while you're gone?"

I raise an eyebrow, surprised she knows how to read. But I assume Lyx helped with that. She was pretty committed to helping her people learn to read and write so they could engage more fully in their world.

Sebastian grins. "Yes, enjoy. But promise to tell me what happens when I get back."

"Deal!" she says and runs out of the room clutching the book against her chest.

I sink into the couch next to the sexy Earth Druid, sliding easily against his heavily muscled body. "That was adorable."

He blushes, actually blushes. "She's a sweet kid. You were right to bring her home."

I lean a head against him. "Thanks. I couldn't just leave her. But I realize we are going to have to figure out what to do with her long term." I glance up at him, catching his gaze. "What happens to kids like her here?"

He frowns. "We don't have a great system for caring for orphans. If no one claims her, or takes her in, she'll end up on the streets where she isn't likely to survive long."

"Shit. That's ridiculous. Why? This is a small, wealthy community with many beings who are nearly immortal or at least long lived. Can't you figure out something better than 'kick 'em to the street and let 'em die'?"

"It is something that needs changed. There are many things that need to change in this world." He pulls me into him and kisses my forehead. "Maybe you'll be the change we need."

"On that note, we should get going. I want to see what Ifi and Elal learned about Lyx's death." I move to stand but Sebastian pulls me back to the couch.

"Not until you've eaten. Liam told me how drained you were last night." He grabs a plate of food from the side table and hands it to me. It's piled high with eggs, bacon, fresh baked bread with a thick pat of butter, and a bowl of berries and cream.

I'm about to tell him I'm not hungry but my stomach rumbles, betraying me.

Sebastian raises an eyebrow and I smile. "Thank you. This looks delicious."

While I eat, Derek and Elijah join us, with Liam following behind holding a baby dragon in one arm and

Alina in the other. "She ate!" he says to Elijah. "You were right. Cooked shark was the way to go." He glances at me in exasperation. "We tried every kind of meat we could think of. Then it occurred to us maybe seafood since she's a water dragon. It took a bit to get to shark." The Fire Druid grins at the dragon in his arms. "You're such a good eater, aren't you?"

"This might be the cutest thing I've ever seen in my life," I say, watching them.

Elijah rises and takes the dragon from Liam. Zara hiccups and spits water all over him, but he just laughs and puts the baby in the crib so he can dry off.

"Here, let me," I say, and I place a hand on his chest and channel fire and air together, drying him in an instant.

"Thank you," he says, his smile almost boyish.

"What will the rest of you do today?" I ask as I take Alina from Liam and give her some love. She pulls at my hair and laughs as she singes the edges with her fire.

"I'm staying with the kids," Liam says. "I thought I'd take them all on a hike and let these two practice their magic somewhere safer."

"I'll join you," Elijah says. "I need to get out of the castle for a bit and enjoy some fresh air. Plus, you'll have your hands full with three kids."

I look to Derek who shrugs. "I'm going to go back to the crime scene to see if I can find any new leads."

"Where's Matilda?" I ask. I haven't seen her around much since Lyx's death.

"She left last night and said she'll be back soon, that she had something to look into," Sebastian says.

With plans in place, Sebastian and I head to the carriage. I could offer to fly us or teleport us, but I'm just learning these abilities and taking another person with me seems risky at best. Besides, there are worse ways in the world to spend a morning than in a carriage with a sexy vampire druid.

I'm about ready to climb into the front, assuming Sebastian will be driving, but he ushers me into the back. "We've got a driver," he says.

"Who? Lily isn't home and everyone else is busy."

I watch, and see the reigns to the horses shift and move through the air... and I smile. "Mable?"

She flicks the reigns to let me know she's there, and Sebastian raises an eyebrow. "You learned her name? How?"

"I have my ways," I tell him with a wink as we crawl into the back of the carriage.

He sits across from me, our knees touching as he leans forward so we're closer. "I'm glad we'll have some time together," he says reaching for my hand.

I take his, squeezing it, and enjoy the feel of our skin touching, even if it's just our palms. "Me too. I feel like we haven't had a minute to ourselves in ages, with all the work we're doing in the new world and now this."

"You've done an incredible job helping build a new community," he says. "I see how the people look at you.

You're a hero to them, and they don't even know you're a Fate."

I laugh at that. "I'm 100% sure they do. Nothing stays a secret in this world for long. Y'all are quite the gossips."

He grins, unable to deny it. "Either way, you've healed a lot of hearts. Mine included."

I know he's still broken about Cole, but it's good to hear some healing has occurred. "This is my home now too. I wasn't exaggerating when I told the Mother of Dragons that this world is part of me now. Or maybe it's more correct to say I'm a part of it. I don't know how it happened exactly, but when I did that spell, it changed something inside me, and added something of me to the fabric of this world. I haven't wanted to admit this to myself, let alone anyone else. But Sebastian, if this world is destroyed, I think I might be destroyed along with it, regardless of where I am. I don't think I'll survive if Amora gets her way."

Sebastian sucks in a breath, his grip on my hands tightening. "How certain are you?"

I drop my head, not wanting to see the heartache in his eyes when I tell him. "I could be wrong, of course, but I don't think I am. I'm... " I look up, unable to pull my gaze from his any longer. "I'm pretty certain. I can feel my life force attached to this world. I know after we found out what I am, we all speculated about my life span. But the more I've used my powers, the more I've felt this connection. I don't think I'll die naturally unless this world does. Which felt like a long time, but now it has the life expectancy of less than two weeks. And so do I."

He's quiet for a few moments, his face hardened against this news. "Maybe Elijah's books can uncover someway to fix this," he says.

"I think the only fix is solving the murder," I say.

"Assuming the Mother of Dragons honors her word," he whispers, pressing his lips into a tight line.

"Why wouldn't she?"

He shrugs. "The dragons follow their own rules. They always have."

"We'll just have to make sure she honors her word this time," I say. "Not just for my sake. We wouldn't be able to evacuate the entire population of this world in time, even if we started now." I pause, thinking. "Should we start now?" I ask. "Should we go public and encourage everyone to leave? To save as many as we can, at least."

He looks pained as he considers the possibility of failure. "If we did that, we would reduce our odds of finding the killer. They would leave, and we wouldn't have any chance of saving the world. And as you said, we still wouldn't be able to evacuate everybody. And where would they go? Not everyone here can pass as human, and even those of us who can would become targets in your world. It would lead to more deaths."

I sigh. "Yeah, I know. But I was hoping I was

wrong. Because I'm worried about our odds. We have so little evidence to go on."

"We'll find more," he says. "We have to."

The carriage begins to slow and I look out the window, surprised to find we have already arrived at the cemetery where the morgue is located.

Unlike the first time I came here, today is a bright day with a light breeze that makes the grass covering the graves sway in synchronicity.

Mable stays with the carriage—presumably, I can't actually see her—and we walk across the cemetery towards the mausoleum when a thought occurs to me. "Are there ghosts here?" It seems the logical place for them.

Sebastian shrugs. "Most likely, why?"

"I just realized Mable might enjoy visiting with others of her kind. They must be a very underrepresented group in the Otherworld."

Sebastian tilts his head and looks around, as if seeing the area with new eyes. "I never actually thought of it like that before."

We approach the mausoleum— a towering gothic building that casts a long shadow over the cemetery with its clustered columns and sharply pointed spires. The stained-glass windows are filled with light today, as the brightness of the Dragon's Breath spill through them.

I pick up my pace when we are close, excited to see the gargoyles that guard the doors.

Okura comes to life first, her stone wings stretching and flexing as she flies down from her perch to land in front of us, a pouch at her stomach heavy with her baby, like a kangaroo.

"Okura!" I run up to her and hug her stony body.

She laughs, and the sound is much like rocks tumbling down a mountain. "It has been too long. And I have heard tales that your truth is finally known, Fate." She bows her head in reverence.

"Oh please, not you too. I'm still just me. How's the baby?"

Akuro lands beside his mate and grins widely. "She is the sun and moon and the stars all in one," he says proudly as Okura pulls the sleeping child from the pouch and hands her to me.

My body sags under the weight of the baby, and Sebastian wraps his arms around me to help support us both. The child blinks, it's eyes large and curious, and then she smiles and reaches out with a little fist to grab my hair.

I laugh. "It seems babies everywhere are all the same."

We spend a few more minutes visiting, with promises to get our families together soon, and they open the doors for us.

As we walk in, Okura says, "We are here if you need us in the upcoming struggles."

I turn towards her. "What do you mean?"

She closes her eyes. "A war is brewing. The Age of

Dragon is coming to an end. Much will be decided in the coming days. Be well, Fate. Count us amongst your allies."

"Thank you," I say, then Sebastian and I continue our walk through the dim halls, and today the smell of death and old flowers is even stronger than normal.

We stop before the large arched double door I recognize from our first visit here, and this time I'm prepared for the scene as we walk in.

Since my powers have manifested so strongly, I'm no longer impacted by the heat and the flames dancing along the edges of the marble walls. It's a large room with dead bodies lying across tables scattered throughout, and long stretches of glass tubing connecting beakers of bubbling liquid in varying shades of green, orange, grey, and purple. I ignore the specimen jars that line the shelves. They creep me out.

Instead, I focus on the two men standing over a body. Both are ablaze in flames that would have seared me in the past. Now, I can walk right up to them and hug them if I want, though I might still burn my clothes off. So I wait for them to de-flame, which they do the moment they see us.

"Eve, Sebastian!" Ifi grins and throws himself into a hug, first with me, then with Sebastian, who looks a little taken back but recovers quickly enough and embraces the Ifrit. I smile at the exchange, glad we have these guys as friends.

While Ifi regales Sebastian in his latest drama, Elal

hugs me, his golden eyes more serious. "Sounds like you have had quite a time with the dragons," he says.

I snort. "That's the understatement of the century. What have you heard?"

Ifi joins us, dragging Sebastian by the hand. "Oh darling, what haven't we heard? Dead dragons, a visit from the Mother of Dragons, your Fate powers going super nova. The Otherworld is getting lit!" he explains with a swivel of his hips.

I burst out laughing and Elal chuckles. "We took a visit to Earth recently. Ifi really liked the socializing on media part. He learned some new words."

"Yeah, I can see that," I say, still chuckling. "But honestly, how do you guys know so much about what happened already? There were only a few of us there."

They share a glance. "We have our ways," Ifi says with a conspiratorial wink.

Elal frowns. "We also know of other, more disturbing things," he says. "End of the world rumors."

I suck in a breath. "How?"

"It is hard to explain. But rest assured this is not common knowledge, and will not become so, not by us at least. While Ifi might be an irredeemable gossip, even he knows when to keep his mouth shut."

I look over at Ifi, who makes a motion to zip up his lips and toss away the key.

"We need to solve this case," I say. "Everything depends on it."

"Then let's get to it, shall we?" Elal says, and with a

flick of his finger he gestures for one of the cooling units to open, and a table comes rolling out with Lyx's body laid out reverently on top, covered in a white sheet.

"We have never autopsied a dragon before," Ifi says, clearly trying to contain his excitement.

"Normally their bodies disintegrate upon death," I say. "Why didn't hers?"

"Our working theory," Elal says, "is that their body remains if their soul was torn from them without their willing consent."

"Does this mean Lyx can't move on? To... wherever dragon souls go when they die?" The afterlife is still a mystery to me, clearly.

"We can't answer that," Elal says.

"Can you tell us what killed her?" Sebastian asks, his voice soft, his demeanor more subdued than normal as he gazes at Lyx.

Elal reaches for a clay sculpture on one of the shelves and holds it up. "Something this shape and size," he says. "I made a mold of the puncture wound and created a sculpture from it."

I take it from his hand and examine it, turning it over in my hand. It's made of grey clay and has a cylinder base that narrows into a sharpened tip with ridges spiraling it. "What does this look like to you?" I ask Sebastian.

He frowns, studying it. "A unicorn horn."

"Right. But there's presumably only one left, and it

wasn't the murder weapon, so where does that leave us?"

"With another mystery to solve in just a few days."

"Can we keep this?" I ask, holding up the sculpture.

"Sure thing," Ifi says. "It's some of my best work." He winks and I grin at him.

"Now, are we ready for the last wish?" Elal asks.

"Yes," Sebastian says softly.

We all step back several feet in anticipation of Ifi's transformation.

He walks over to Lyx's body and stands by her side, then bursts into flames. The fire burns brightly and Sebastian shifts uncomfortably, sweating. I reach for his hand and use my water and air magic to dampen the heat for him. He pulls me closer to him and kisses my head as Ifi begins chanting in his own language. As before, his voice becomes layered with other voices, the vibration of them shaking the room. It feels like an earthquake moving through the mausoleum and then a loud screeching fills the air. Flames dance against the marble walls and ceilings, and the body of Lyx begins to shake as Ifi's magic fills her, animating her from within.

She sits up and turns to us, light filling her body, her soul returning to her eyes. She looks at Sebastian first. "Son," she says, "Keep your light close."

Then she looks at me and her face contorts in terror. "The mother must be stopped."

I expect her to drop back to the table, dead once

again, but instead, she bursts into explosions of light that go off like fireworks in the contained space.

As vials of liquid begin exploding, I grab Sebastian and put up a shield, using a blend of light, air, water and darkness. It seems to do the trick as sizzling chemicals splash against the shield and slide off harmlessly, and projectile balls of fire and light crash into it and fizzle out. I feel the hits to my magic but withstand it easily as Elal and Ifi rush to contain the damage.

Eventually the light show dies down and then Lyx's body bursts into dust and disappears, leaving nothing but a massive mess behind.

"That was fire!" Ifi says in awe.

Sebastian looks confused, so I clarify. "It's a meme thing. It means cool."

"Fire means cool? That wasn't any more clarifying."

I snort. "Welcome to my world."

THE NOTE

We are weaned from our timidity
*   In the flush of love's light*
*   we dare be brave*
*   And suddenly we see*
*   that love costs all we are*
*   and will ever be.*
*   Yet it is only love*
*   which sets us free.*
*   ~Maya Angelou, Touched by an Angel*

SEBASTIAN and I wait in Ifi and Elal's private quarters while they put out the last of the fires in their lab. I offered to help, but they insisted there were too many variables to allow other magic to interfere.

I look around in surprise at their very modern studio situated upstairs in the mausoleum. It's all leather and steel, tasteful and sparse, juxtaposed against stone walls and marble floors. Their kitchen is small but gourmet, with some definite black trade gadgets from my world. "How do they even make a cappuccino machine work without electricity?" I ask.

"Magic?" Sebastian postures as he takes a seat on the leather sofa.

He's been pretty quiet since we got up here, so I take a seat next to him and place a hand on his knee. "You okay?" I ask.

He grunts.

"So that's a no," I say. "I know you all have a history with the Light Dragon. Do you want to talk about it? This must be hard for you."

It was unusual that she had two 'last wishes'. Not to mention that she blew up after. The Ifrits look shook—as Ifi might now say with his new grasp of earth modern lingo.

"She was my mentor," he finally says. "Before I became a Druid."

I nod. "I knew you'd been close at one point, before your falling out."

"Falling out," he says, with a bitter undertone to his words. "Yes. We certainly did. She turned her backs on us—on me—because she didn't like the direction the Order was going."

"Because of the Fates," I say, and guilt floods me even though I'm not really the same person as back then. At least I don't feel like I am.

"Yes, in part. There were a lot of complicated politics at play. And then Cole did what he did, and she sided with him against the Order and the Fates, severing ties with us all, just as Cole did."

"And you lost your brother and your mentor all at once," I say. "That must have been heartbreaking."

"I spent the first two decades of my life being trained by her to prepare for my initiation into the Order. Hours every day which became longer the older I grew. She taught me the history, the lore, the use of my powers, the control of my emotion. She was the only mother I really ever knew."

"Who were your parents?" I ask, shocked that I've never had this conversation with any of them.

"I don't really remember them," he says, his eyes losing focus as his mind is drawn into the past. "My brothers and I were born on a farm. Our parents were poor, and when they discovered we had powers, they feared us cursed by demons. The Druidic Order heard about us and sent Lyx to acquire us. My parents were more than happy to take the gold to get rid of us. Hell, had they had any money to begin with, I think they would have paid to have us taken away."

"Did you all develop your gifts at the same time?" I ask, my heart breaking for the little boy whose parents didn't want him.

"Strangely yes," he says. "It was after Cole was born, once he developed his light powers at age two. Somehow that triggered it for all of us. Liam burned down part of the barn that day—which likely explains why our parents thought we were a curse. Our magic was so raw and untapped, we caused only grief for them."

I reach for his hand and hold it in mine. "Did you ever see them again?"

He looks away, unable to meet my eyes. "Their village was destroyed when we were cursed and lost control of our powers." He pauses, and the weight of his words hit me with a visceral force. "That's when we decided to end our lives."

Now tears are burning my eyes, and I let them fall. I know how awful that time was for them. I remember the pain when they first told me what happened. But this... this is so much worse than I even imagined. I want him to know that I see his pain and hold space for him.

He lifts his free hand and runs the pad of his thumb across my cheekbone, stealing my tear. "It has been many, many lifetimes, and I am not who I was then."

His hand, still caressing my cheek, moves to the back of my head, his fingers tangling in my hair as he pulls me forward.

With an urgent need he claims my lips, pulling me onto his lap as he does.

Like an earthquake, everything shifts between us, and I adjust my legs, straddling him on the couch to get closer. His hands fall to my ass, pulling me even nearer, fingers digging into my flesh as he deepens our kiss.

I nip at his lower lip and he growls and hardens beneath me, pressing himself between my legs. An agonizing need crashes through me, creating a temporary amnesia to where we are.

It's not until the door opens that we both remember we are guests at the Ifrits home. Startled, I roll off his lap into the couch next to him and he casually covers his pants with a throw pillow.

I can feel the blood rushing to my face and know within moments I'll look like a disheveled beet.

Ifi raises an eyebrow at us as he walks in. "Looks like you two have been having fun with out us," he teases.

They both left their white lab coats downstairs and Ifi is dressed in torn jeans and a band t-shirt. Elal is wearing more of a Renaissance style outfit of dark leggings with a long sleeved shirt and doublet. Elal heads to the pantry and pulls out a bottle of wine. "Ifi, leave them be." He glances at us. "Care for a glass?"

"Sure," I say. "Thank you."

Elal pours four glasses and brings them over, then they both take a seat across from us.

"Was the lab too badly destroyed?" I ask, sipping my drink.

"Thank the fires, no." Elal says.

"But it's an unholy mess nonetheless," Ifi interjects,

already on his second glass of wine. "Still, worth it. Who else can say a dragon blew up in their morgue."

Elal shoots Ifi a glance that is absolutely couple-speak for, "she was their friend, don't be such an ass." And his face changes to, "by the fires you're right, what a nob I'm being."

At least that's how I interpret it. But Ifi stammers an apology. "I can be an insensitive prat sometimes."

"It's fine," Sebastian says, finally able to move the pillow off his lap. "It was pretty remarkable. What do you think caused that?"

"My best guess is when Ifi pulled her dying wish from her, it cleared her soul of the karmic energy to move on," Elal says. "Or another magic interfered because they didn't want her sharing anything more."

My breath hitches at his words. "Is that possible? Could she have said more? I thought you only got one wish, but she said two."

"Oh the dead can say whatever they damn well please," says Ifi. "They just usually don't have much umph left in them, if you catch my drift. But the Light Dragon, she was one of the most powerful beings alive. I'd bet she could have solved her own murder if she could've spoken longer."

"But who could have done that to her?" I ask. "What kind of power?"

"That's why that particular theory seems most unlikely," Elal says, casting a frown at Ifi. "Because it shouldn't be possible. Not with the spells and counter spells on this place, plus Okura and Akuro guarding it. Likely she'd fulfilled her death wish and moved on."

Once we are done with our drinks, Sebastian and I stand to take our leave. "It's been so good seeing you again. Come over for dinner sometime," I say at the door.

Elal gives me a hug and Ifi screeches and bursts into flames, startling us all.

"What the hell?" Sebastian says, rushing out of the way of the flames.

Ifi simmers down and apologizes. "I've been having hot flashes lately," he says. "Especially when I remember something important."

"I'm thinking hot flashes mean something different for you than they do for my world," I say. "But regardless, what did you remember?"

Ifi heads over to a desk and pulls out an envelope. "We were asked to give this to you, and only you."

Curious, I open it, and find a note written in heavy script font with dripping black ink.

MEET me at Landal's Tomb when you get this. I have information that could help you. Come alone or I won't be there. ~Dath'Racul

"WHAT'S LANDAL'S TOMB?" I ask.

"Doesn't matter," Sebastian says, reading over my shoulder. "You're not going."

"You know I have to," I say. "Too much is at stake and we know too little right now."

"Then I'm coming with you." Sebastian crosses his arms stubbornly over his chest.

"No, you're not. He won't show if you do. Besides, I think I've proven I can take care of myself."

"Uh oh," Ifi singsongs. "A lovers' quarrel. But they do make the best make-up sex."

Elal shushes his lover and I blush for the second time today. Sebastian looks away, and I know we are both thinking about being in bed together for the first time. That moment needs to happen sooner rather than later.

"He could be the killer," Sebastian says.

"That seems unlikely. The dagger isn't the murder weapon."

"Dragons don't need a horn, remember?"

I sigh, wishing we had more clues. But that's exactly why I need to meet with him.

"Even if he didn't do it, he's dangerous," says Sebastian.

"I faced off his mother, I think I can handle him," I say. "Besides I'm not going there to fight him, just to hear what he has to say." I turn to the Ifrits. "Where, and what, is Landal's Tomb?" I ask again.

Sebastian falls into a melancholy sulk while Elal answers my question.

"Landal's Tomb is where one of the three original Fates was buried."

My ears perk up at that. "Are there tombs for all three Fates?" I ask. In my mind I'm wondering if *I'm* buried somewhere, which is such a weird and creepy thing to contemplate.

"Nope," Ifi says, linking his arm through Elal's. The bigger Ifrit pulls Ifi closer, their bodies conforming to each other's as they speak. "She was the only one whose body was found after they disappeared. The other two were presumed dead, but no one knows for sure what happened to them."

"How did she die?" I ask.

"She was murdered," Ifi whispers, as if this is top secret information. "But no one knows by whom. However, there aren't many beings that can kill a fate. The list is short."

"Ifi," Elal says sternly.

"What? It's not like she can hear us. Not here."

Elal frowns. "It's best not to speak ill of her regardless."

"Speak ill of who?" I ask, though I'm beginning to suspect who they're talking about.

They share a concerned glance and Elal sighs. "All I can say is this. Be careful with the dragons. And go to that meeting."

Sebastian grumbles but doesn't argue.

"I need to know where it is," I say.

"Well you're in luck, darling," Ifi says, throwing an

arm over my shoulder and walking me to the window. He points across the field of gravestones to the far end where a larger structure stands. "That's the entrance. The rest is underground. Go in and follow the steps down. You'll find what you're looking for."

I glance at Sebastian. "Will you wait here for me?" I ask.

"I guess I have to," he says, reluctantly sinking back into the couch.

Elal holds the door open for me, but I shake my head. "I've got a faster way to travel these days."

I close my eyes and think of the location Ifi just showed me, tapping into my darkness, and then I disintegrate.

I land just where I plan, outside the door to Landal's Tomb. It's getting easier to do this teleporting thing, which pleases me.

Vines and moss cover the stone structure before me with lifetimes of growth, and creepers hang down over the entrance, covering the door. Though it looks to have been recently disturbed.

I push through and open the entrance. It squeaks and cracks as it opens and the scent of mildew and dust clogs my throat. I cough, choking a bit before I remember I can use air magic to clear some of this up. A flick of my wrist and I can take a deep breath with more ease. That handled, I navigate down the stairs, casting a ball of light on my palm to guide the way.

Cobwebs catch in my hair and something squishes

under my feet, but I don't look to see what. I don't really want to know.

When I finally get to the bottom, I enter a cavernous space full of candles. The room has a tall ceiling, and in the center is a sculpture of a beautiful woman draped in a see-through gown. The stonework is incredible, truly magnificent. It's as if her soul was brought to life, and a chill runs down my spine as I stare at her form.

In another life, she and I were friends.

Or sisters.

I'm unclear.

But we were close.

Who were the other Fates? What were they like? I have so many questions I can never hope to get answered.

"She's stunning, is she not? I tried to capture her essence."

I turn to see Dath'Racul leaning against the stone wall studying me, his long red wing-cape draped over his broad shoulders, his eyes hooded in shadows.

"You sculpted this?"

"I did," he says, stepping forward, into the flicking candlelight. "She was my lover. When she died, a piece of me died with her."

THE FORBIDDEN

"Your task is not to seek for love, but merely to seek and find all the barriers within yourself that you have built against it."

~Rumi

HIS WORDS LEAVE ME STUNNED. "LOVER?"

"Does that surprise you, Miss Oliver? That I would be capable of love?" He steps closer, now standing inches from me, his massive form towering over me, his golden dragon eyes studying me with a penetrating intelligence that is unnerving. The candlelight plays off his deep burnt red skin, giving him a demonic quality that actually seems to amplify his attractiveness.

"We are, all of us, capable of love. The depth of that love is determined by the depth of our own souls," I say.

He tilts his head, studying me. "I was surprised to learn you were one of the Fates," he says in a non-sequitur. "But the more I study you, the more I see the wisdom of your past bleeding through the frailness of your small human life."

"That almost sounded like a compliment," I say. "If you keep working at it, I think you'll nail it one of these days."

His lips twitch as if he's tempted to smile, but he resists the impulse. "I wasn't sure you would attend this meeting."

"Why wouldn't I?" I ask. "I'm committed to solving this murder. I want to see the Light Dragon's killer brought to justice, and I obviously don't want to see your mother destroy the Otherworld."

"Yes. You are an altruist through and through. Tell me, do you share the ruthlessness of the Maiden Fate of the past? Will you cross lines drawn in blood to do what you think is right?"

His gaze bores into me as if he's trying to pillage my soul of all its secrets. Secrets even I'm not privy to.

"Whatever choices we make, whatever actions we take to protect, to guide, to lead, to bring justice, they should not and cannot undermine our basic goodness and decency, otherwise what is it all for?"

He steps back from me, half his face falling into shadows as he does. "So you would let the innocent die if the alternative required acting in a way against your conscious?"

I glance up at the sculpture, letting my hand study the delicate artistry of it. "This is the first representation I've seen of a Fate where her face is shown," I say, changing the subject. "Why is that?"

I've noticed he's studiously avoided looking at the image of his lover, but now that he does, his eyes soften briefly. "The Fates never showed their faces. Not to the dragons, not to my mother, not to anyone. They were more myth than anything." He turns his attention back to me. "Which is why no one knew who you were," he says.

"Do you mean I would have looked like this in my past life?" I ask. "I thought with reincarnation you come back in a new body, new look and all that?"

"Perhaps under normal circumstances. But you are not normal. You are not reincarnated. You are a fate reborn. You'd do well to remember that. You may not wish to face your past deeds, but they remain part of you regardless." He looks away, his face showing a moment of brokenness that surprises me. "We all must deal with the consequences of who we were, whether we recognize that person now or not."

"And who were you, once upon a time?" I ask in a whisper.

The air around us feels heavy with the weight of the past, with ghosts that still haunt us both, even if I can no longer remember them.

"A man in love," he says without looking at me.

"Who didn't want to see what my choices would do to the one I loved."

I look back at Landal, who looks suspended in time, mid-dance, her body twirling, the sheer dress she wears flowing around her, her head turned to glance over her shoulder at someone, her face lit up with joy and love.

"What was she like?" I ask.

"Do you not remember anything?" he asks with a frown.

"Not really. It hasn't been that long that I really knew who I was. And I've only had flashes of memory. Nothing I can hold onto. But I feel her inside me, writhing like a living thing trying to escape. Sometimes I don't know where I begin and she ends," I admit, surprising even me. I haven't articulated these thoughts to myself, let alone anyone else. I never imagined Dath'Racul would be the one I could confess to.

By the look on his face, he didn't either.

I expect a sharp retort, a biting insult, a cutting jibe. But instead, he walks over to a bench I didn't notice before. One in the shadows, but that has a perfect view of the Landal.

He sits, and gestures that I should join him.

There is barely enough room for both of us, and our thighs press together as I take my seat, sending a jolt of electricity through my skin. My fire magic flares, being this close to the Fire Dragon, and his eyes widen, suggesting he feels it too.

"Your powers have grown substantially since we met at the Collector's party," he says. "I was a bit distracted that day with my mother that I didn't feel the full weight of it then, despite your rather impressive grandstanding."

I ignore the grandstanding comment, because I can be a bigger person. "The spell with Ava'Kara seems to have unlocked what was trapped in me."

I swear his eyes seem to mist over when I mention her name.

"I wish she would have talked to us before sacrificing herself. We could have found another way."

I turn to him, my face hardening. "I think she didn't go to you because you seemed determined to use your power and position to take advantage of the fear that people lived in. You stoked that fear and used it to make yourself stronger. She wanted to help. But you wanted control."

"I know it may seem that way in your minuscule and insignificant human life of what? Twenty or thirty years?" he says, his voice hardening. "But I created a world for the people you say I just want to control. It was Landal and I who talked my brothers and sisters as well as the other Fates into forming the foundation of the Otherworld. You cannot possibly know what that entails. What responsibility that involves."

There was a lot to unpack in his little speech, but my tolerance for his dismissive attitude had worn thin.

"Listen up, Racul, can I call you Racul?" I say, not

waiting for him to answer. "Things will go a lot better between us if you drop this bullshit about my age, okay? You think because you've been around a few more years you're so much wiser? So much better? And yet here we are, dealing with dead dragons and a world apocalypse because you and your sibs can't find a way to get along." His eyes narrow at that, but I don't give him time to respond. I'm too pissed. "You keep this world stuck in the dark age. You prohibit advancement. You don't take care of the most vulnerable of your population. You disparage anyone who disagrees with you. You don't listen to anyone but yourself. You've become so myopic you don't even see that you are destroying the very thing you created."

When I finish, I'm nearly out of breath. My cheeks are flushed and I'm riled up.

I wait expectantly for him to say something.

But instead, he leans over and kisses me.

What the hell?

His lips are hot, searing, and burn straight through me, and I respond to him for a moment, drawn into his fire and power, but then I regain my senses, pull back and slap him across the face.

I think it hurts my hand more than his face. And he doesn't look at all phased or apologetic.

"What the hell was that!"

My body is tingling, and I don't even know what to do with all the emotions roiling through me like lava.

"It has been a long time since a woman spoke to me like that," he says, glancing at the statue again.

"That doesn't entitle you to my lips," I say, slightly softening but still low key pissed.

"Forgive me. I am too accustomed to getting what I want." He doesn't look sorry, though. Just arrogant.

"No shit. That's abundantly clear, and part of the problem. You created this world, but you don't own the people in it," I say. "You have to change with the times. Learn and grow. I'm always so stunned at how little self-development you long-lived beings accomplish. Humans have got you beat in that, for your information. For all that you criticize our puny mortal life spans, most of us bust our asses to grow, and learn, and accomplish as much as we can in that time. You, for all your lofty greatness, have done what in the last thousand years? How have you changed? Grown? What have you learned?"

He looks lost in thought, and then his lips twitch into a smile. "I was about to say that Landal would have liked you, and then I realized you two were close once. She shared your zeal for the downtrodden and abused. This world was actually her idea. She was tired of seeing so many of the magical community hunted and killed just for being different. She had a vision of a world where all could live in safety."

His words give me pause. "Did... did you know *me*... the me back then?"

"Only casually. I never saw your face, as I said. Or

the Crone Fate. She spoke about the two of you from time to time, but Fate business and Dragon business were things we didn't share with each other freely. When we were together, we tried to let go of that and just be us."

"How did she die?" I ask, recalling what Ifi said before I came here.

Racul looks at Landal's statue, his expression almost heartbreaking. It is the look of a man trying hard to control emotions that he's suppressed for too many years. Emotions of love, pain, loss, betrayal, anger.

On impulse, I take his hand. It burns hot in my own but doesn't hurt me. He looks down at our hands, and I think he's about to pull away, but instead he squeezes mine and turns his gaze back to me.

"The truth of her death has never been uncovered," he says. "But I know what happened."

I bite my tongue to keep from asking more questions. I have a feeling if I wait, he'll speak more freely than if I interrogate him. He looks as if he's standing on the edge of his past, waiting to fall into it.

The silence lingers between us. Something scurries in the shadows across the room, disturbing the cobwebs. Dust mites dance in the fractals of light cast by the candles. The stagnant air settles around us. Still I wait.

When he finally speaks, his words are hushed, his deep voice laden with pain.

"My mother is a formidable being, as you have seen."

I can't help but snort at that. Understatement of the year.

"She did not support the formation of this world. She feels that dragons are the only pure bloods, and any other beings of magic are bastards, weakened by lesser blood. Not worth our time or energy. Certainly not worth creating an entire world for, abandoning our own in the process."

He pauses, swallowing, lost in thought. "She did not know about my relationship with Landal. Just that we had worked together to convince the others to join our quest. She was livid, but what could she do? We outnumbered her, and she knew if she pushed too hard, she would lose us entirely. So she relented."

He shifts in his seat, pulling my hand closer to him, still holding it tightly as if it's a lifeline for him. On instinct, I send a thread of my magic, the blend of all the elements, to him and I see his skin glow at the contact for just a moment before it fades.

He gapes at me, astonished. "Thank you."

I nod.

He clears his throat. "We celebrated when the world formed. We rejoiced when beings entered here, forming towns, homes, lives. We did our best to set up a fair and just system to manage the growing population. The Fates did not take an active role here, as they still had commitments on your world, but Landal came as frequently as she could to be with me."

I can feel the story shift, feel the tale turn dark as his eyes themselves darken in the telling. "My mother discovered our relationship a few thousand years ago. It all came to a head at a very unfortunate time in our world. There was already a... war with the unicorns. Strange things happening. And then..."

My breath hitches. "Did you mother kill Landal?" I ask.

His golden eyes fill with tears that turn to steam before they can find release. "I've never had proof. But yes, she did."

"Racul," I say, my voice more tender than it was. "Why did you ask me to come here?"

"When I built this memorial for Landal, I had it spelled. My mother does not know of it, and cannot hear or see anything that goes on within these walls. She will not even see that it exists. She will only see a vacant stretch of cemetery land," he says.

"Why?" I ask.

"Because I needed one place in the universe where I was free from her. I am the eldest of my siblings, and until I met Landal and we decided to create the Otherworld, I was in line to succeed my mother in our own world, where only dragons live. We are not the only dragons that exist, but we are the only dragons of the royal line. I was to be king. When I relinquished that to come here, my mother disowned me, and I have never lived up to her expectations since. Similarly, Lyx has always defied her. Lyx had a big heart, too big. I feared for her. I was angry at her for leaving the Council, for becoming the Beggar Queen as they called her. Not because she was helping the poor, as many think. But because I knew she was putting herself at risk with our mother."

"Are you saying...."

"I'm saying, I think my mother killed Lyx for defying her, just as she killed Landal for my defiance. And I think you were never meant to solve this murder. I'm saying, the world is going to end in less than a fortnight, and you should leave now."

Shit. Double triple shit.

"Racul, I can't. The spell... it made me a part of this world. I will die if it is destroyed."

His face shifts subtly, and I'm surprised to see that he actually cares about my fate.

"Then you need to find a way to stop my mother. I will help. But first, we need to go to the Ancient Library. It might hold information, or at least some sort of evidence that could help us take her down."

"What's the Ancient Library?" I ask, my pulse quickening.

"It is a secret place my mother built to hide all her secrets," he says simply.

"Why haven't you already gone?" I ask, my heart fluttering at the thought that we might have a new lead.

"Because only the Fates and my mother are able to open it. I need your help."

I can see how hard it is for him to admit this. "Okay, I'm in. When?"

"Tomorrow morning," he says. "I will pick you up."

"I'll be ready," I say, knowing the Night brothers are going to *looooove* this. Not.

"We will find a way to defeat my mother and save this world. Together."

THE LIBRARY

"I said to the night,
"If you are in love with the moon,
it is because you never stay for long."
The night turned to me and said,
"It is not my fault. I never see the Sun,
how can I know that love is endless?"
~Rumi

DATH and I leave the tomb together and he takes my hand once more as we stand outside. "Apologies for stealing a kiss. You reminded me so much of her, it was... well, it doesn't matter. You're right. You're not mine to claim."

My heart feels a pang of regret that his relationship ended the way it did. It seems he's not found love again since. "It's not too late to find companionship once more," I say. "You have a long life ahead of you. Let yourself open up to something new again. I think she would want that for you."

He tilts his head. "Is that from memory?"

"No," I say. "But it's what I would want for someone that I loved. It's what I would want for you."

"Be safe, Miss Oliver. I will see you tomorrow."

He pulls away from me and transforms into a giant red dragon, fire sparking from his mouth. He gives me a brief nod and flies away, disappearing into the Dragon's Breath covering sky.

I glance back at the mausoleum where I know Sebastian is sitting in Ifi and Elal's home, worried sick. Poor guy. I close my eyes and teleport to their apartment.

I rematerialize... awkwardly, landing in Sebastian's lap, who is still sitting on the couch where I left him.

He grunts, catching me and preventing me from hitting my head on the edge of the metal and glass coffee table.

"I'm so sorry," I say, my arms wrapped around his neck to keep from falling.

He tightens his grip on me rather than letting me go. "I'm not," he says softly, his forest green eyes locked on mine.

"We have not stopped talking about you," Ifi says, with an excited clap of his hands. "Your powers are on fleek!"

I laugh and scoot off Sebastian to stand and stretch. "Thanks."

I give the Earth Druid a meaningful glance. "We should head home. There's a lot to discuss."

He raises an eyebrow and stands while I hug the guys and thank them for everything. "Any luck on the baby front?" I ask, knowing they are trying to adopt.

Ifi grins. "We might have a lead. But it's too soon to tell. Crossing fingers and toes. The need is real. My biological clock is ticking."

"Calm yourself, love. We are immortal. There is no clock," Elal says.

"Okay, Boomer," Ifi says, and I nearly die.

"Ifi, love, that's not quite what that means," I say, through fits of giggles. "But solid effort."

We leave and I'm still laughing as we head back to the carriage. "He's a crack up."

"They are quite entertaining," Sebastian agrees. "Now, tell me, what happened."

"First off, you're not going to like a lot of what I say, but I need you to chill, okay?"

He glares at me.

"Sebastian, I need your word."

With a huff he relents. "Fine. Tell me."

We climb into the carriage and Mable spurs the horses into movement.

Once we are on our way, I tell him everything. Including the kiss.

Sebastian clutches his fist but doesn't say anything until I'm done.

"I know if I forbid you to go to the Ancient Library tomorrow, you'll just do it anyways," he says after a moment of silence.

I smile. "You're finally learning."

He narrows his eyes at me but continues. "You and Elijah should hit the books tonight to see what you can learn about it before you go. There might be traps. Spells. Best to get as much information as you can, for protection at least."

I'm about to say that Racul will be there too, but I don't think Sebastian will find that as reassuring as I intend it to be. Quite the contrary, so I keep my mouth shut.

When we get home, Lily arrives at the same time, and she grins when she sees us.

"I've missed your face," I say, reaching to hug her as she approaches.

"Yours too," she says. "Which is why I thought I should come home, at least for a few days."

I tilt my head at her. "Is everything okay with Kaya?"

"Oh totally. She's going to swing by later to stay in my tree for a bit. Seems only fair."

"That's wonderful," I say.

We enter the house together and Liam and Elijah greet us with exhausted enthusiasm.

"Thank the gods you all are home. These kids are running us ragged."

Lily laughs. "Kaya and I can take care of them tonight. Give you a break."

The gratitude evident on their faces makes me laugh out loud. "Come on guys, it couldn't have been that bad."

"Alina burned down a tree. And Zara nearly flooded a village."

I gasp and Elijah raises a hand. "I stopped her. I used wind to move the water, but now we have a new lake."

"How's Ana?" I ask.

"Already in bed," Liam says. "She was lovely, though a little sad that her 'friend' hadn't come to see her recently."

I shake my head sadly. "She must have led such a hard, lonely life. At least when I lost my dad, I still had Adam. We might have been in and out of foster homes, but we always had each other. Poor girl. Even her imaginary friend isn't always there for her."

Liam nods. "I think being here is good for her. She's surrounded by a family and love. Healing will take time, but like the body, the soul can heal with the right ingredients."

I've always been intrigued by the juxtaposition of Liam's hot-headed anger, and his heart and skill for healing. He really should have gotten the water element, but he's made it work.

"How are the babies?" I ask.

Liam rolls his eyes dramatically. "They will be the death of me. I thought one was a handful. Two is triple the damage, especially when one can turn into a dragon and fly."

Elijah chuckles. "I had to keep using air power to prevent Zara from flying away entirely."

"Sounds like you two had an exciting day. How about we all get dinner and I'll tell you my news?"

Dinner for them would be blood. But I needed real food. As if to prove my point, my stomach begins to rumble.

"Where are the kids?" Lily asks.

"I got them to bed, but those babies won't stay asleep. I tried separating them but then they scream and cry, so... I don't know what to do," Liam says, looking despondent.

Lily giggles. "I'll take care of it." She heads upstairs while we settle into the library.

Elijah brings me a tray with steak, potatoes, green beans and a fresh salad. "This is normal meat, yes? Nothing weird... or talking?" You really can't be too careful about the meat in this world, I've learned.

"I would never feed you anything else," he assures me. I smile and thank him and dig in.

"Where's Derek," I ask?

Liam shrugs. "He hasn't come home yet. Hopefully he's chasing down a lead."

This is when cell phones would be super handy. I

don't often think of the things I gave up to live in the Otherworld, but every once in a while the thought crosses my mind when a modern convenience could solve a host of problems.

Also, I miss him. After last night, I find myself thinking about his lips... and other body parts, at random. I'm looking forward to another round with the Water druid.

Pulling my mind out of the... water...I tell the remaining brothers about my meeting with Racul.

They are stunned silent.

"I told her this is a bad idea," Sebastian says.

None disagree with him, but I see the spark of intrigue in Elijah's eyes, so I pounce. "Have you heard of the Ancient Library?" I ask the Air Druid.

"Not specifically, but there have always been rumors of a secret library filled with cursed spells and dangerous magic. If you really do get in, please take notes on everything you find and bring back as much as you can. That's a gold mine." He pauses, his pale blue eyes full of thought. "I should go with you," he says finally.

"I wish you could, but that wasn't part of the deal. I'm not sure Racul will be okay with anyone else coming."

" Racul isn't to be trusted," Liam says, his eyes blazing.

Oh the irony that the Fire Druid and Fire Dragon, both sexy, arrogant hot heads, hate each other so much.

But Racul did try to execute Liam for a crime he didn't commit not so long ago, so I don't blame him.

"This isn't about trust. He doesn't want the world to end. Neither do I."

Sebastian opens his mouth to say something, but I shake my head. Not right now. I don't want to explain to everyone else what's at stake. I probably shouldn't have even told him, but I needed someone to confide in. I won't deny I'm scared. But I'm not trying to save the world to just save my own life. There are many lives on the line, and I need the Nights focused on that, not on me.

Sebastian clamps his mouth shut and frowns at me.

"It sounds to me like Racul has mommy issues," Liam says, still pissed. About the kiss or the whole thing, I have no idea. Probably everything. It doesn't take much to rile him up, in or out of the bedroom.

"That may be, but if the Mother of Dragons is behind it all, how do we handle this? You guys nearly had a fit at the thought of me going up against her, but we will have to if she tries to destroy the Otherworld. So, any ideas how to defeat her?"

Elijah stands. "I need to do some more research. On the library and on dragons. When reading up on how to take care of Zara, I came across some references to other books which I have since acquired yet haven't had a chance to read. I'll get on that now."

I'm done with my dinner and set the tray aside, standing. "I'll join you. Two eyes are better than one."

He smiles. "Your mind—and company—will be much appreciated."

As we leave, Sebastian pulls me aside, holding my hand. "Why don't you want me telling them?"

"Because they need to focus, and so do we. We'll tell them if we have no choice."

"Fine. But we have to tell them eventually."

"Not if we save the world," I say with a wink and a nonchalance I'm totally faking.

I find Elijah already bent over a stack of books at a table in his office library. I sit across from him and without looking, he pushes a pile to me. I take a quill and parchment and open up the first book in the pile. I basically have a photographic memory, so the notes are more for Elijah than for me.

I speed read the first book, but nothing stands out as helpful other than one story of a dragon killed by its own reflection in a children's myth. It seems sketchy at best as reliable information, but I take notes anyways and move on.

Several hours pass and my neck cramps before I set another book down to stretch. Elijah is gone, and reappears moments later with a plate of fresh chocolate chip cookies. "I know they're your favorite. I thought you could use the sugar."

"You are my favorite person in the world right now," I say as I munch on one. "Seriously, I wish you could still enjoy food. These are the bomb."

When only crumbs are left on the plate, Elijah stands behind me and massages my shoulders.

"Oh my god that feels amazing."

"You're tense. I shouldn't have kept you up this late. You have an early morning."

"I know, but this is important. One of these books might hold some useful information," I say. Though so far none have yielded much. My parchment only has a few notes on it and none particularly relevant.

His massage finishes, leaving me much more relaxed, and I stand and lean against the table to face him, half sitting on it as I do. "We have the unicorn dagger," I say. "That could kill her, couldn't it? If it came to it?"

He takes a step closer to me, and I'm reminded again of how delicious Elijah really is, with his silver blue eyes and perfect porcelain skin. He's tall and lean, with a chiseled body that would be the envy of any underwear model. When he takes a step closer to me, it becomes a little harder to breathe.

"Theoretically it could," he says. "But the challenge would be getting it into her heart without her killing you first. From all accounts, she is the most powerful being in the world. In any world actually."

He comes closer still, and lifts a finger to wipe at my lower lip. "You had a bit of chocolate there," he says softly, his eyes dropping to study me—all of me.

"I know I've told you this before," he says. "But I've never known a woman—or anyone—like you. And I'm not talking about your powers. I'm talking about your mind. And your heart." He pauses, as if considering his words. "I have lived in my head so long, it has distanced me from my emotions. I considered them a weakness to overcome, rather than a necessary part of my being."

He brushes a stray hair out of my face as he studies me. "But you. You have the mind of a genius. Unparalleled. Even by me, if I'm being honest. And yet it hasn't numbed you to your heart. You still care. You are still full of compassion. And... Eve, you made me feel. You made my heart beat again—metaphorically of course."

I chuckle at that. "Of course."

"What I'm trying to say is, I know I'm not the most expressive or romantic person, but I am drawn to you like I have never been to anyone before in my very long life. I hope you know I would do anything for you. Sacrifice anything for you."

And in that moment, I know that if the Air Druid doesn't kiss me soon, I will throw him to the table and make shit happen myself.

But he surprises me and makes the first move, leaning in to claim my lips.

The touch is just a breath between us, stirring my air magic as he deepens the kiss into something that blows through me and leaves me weak-kneed. He lifts me up to the table and spreads my legs to press himself between them as he runs his hands down my back, clutching my ass to pull me closer.

His breath hitches as my hand slides down between us.

Then it's my turn to lose my breath as I feel the length and girth of what's being offered.

He grins into my mouth. "I take it that's satisfactory?"

"It'll do," I joke, and he lifts me from the table, my legs straddling him, his muscles bulging as he carries me to the middle of his office where a bear skin rug is spread out before the fire. He lowers me to the rug carefully and once he does, he pulls off his shirt.

I admire the ripples of muscles and run my hands over his abs, then raise my own arms so he can help me undress.

"Gods you are beautiful," he says as my breasts are freed.

I lay back as he tugs off my pants and underwear, and I return the favor until we are both naked, the lights of the fire dancing over our skin.

He lies beside me and uses his mouth and hands to memorize every inch of my body. With air magic he teases and tickles my most sensitive spots, creating a delicious tension within me that builds and builds like a tornado at my center.

Then I take control, pressing his back to the rug as I straddle him, teasing his hardness before I move up his body to feel his tongue.

And feel it I do.

He takes me in his mouth with such passion and

attention to detail that I have to pace myself to keep from losing it too soon.

Finally, I can no longer handle more, and my body is pushed over the edge, into sheer bliss.

Without hesitation, he readjusts my hips to his own, and as I slide onto him, I moan and melt into the pleasure he brings with his every thrust. His hands hold my hips, while his magic explores my breasts.

On impulse, I channel my own air magic and use it to push us off the ground, so that we are both hovering in flight as we make love. He joins his magic to mine and the intimacy and connection from this shared elemental power is intoxicating. I feel drunk on it, on him.

When I fall over the edge again, he joins me and together we soar.

We slowly fall back to the carpet and with deep satiation, fall asleep in each other's arms.

THE PAST

The changing heart turns evermore
   And changes that of more and more
   Now I see forever lost
   These broken things of little cost
   ~Neil Stevens, The Changing Heart

I WAKE in Elijah's arms, his breath on my neck as he spoons me in front of a dying fire. I send a spark of fire magic to fan the flames, giving the room a much-needed burst of warmth, then turn over to face him, our legs entangling underneath a feathered blanket. He must have brought it at some point in the night. I kiss him tenderly on his lips, and he stirs, waking, kissing me back.

A banging on the office door interrupts our moment. "Derek's home and has news," Liam shouts through the door, then takes off down the hall, probably to get everyone else.

I groan my disappointment and pull out of his arms reluctantly. "Guess we'd better get dressed," I say.

He sighs. "I prefer you this way," he admits with a boyish grin. "But I suppose you are right. I wish we'd found more that could help you today. I'll keep looking while you're gone."

I kiss him and let my lips linger as he cups my ass and grows hard against my stomach. "You're not making this easy," I say against his mouth.

"I blame you entirely," he says, smiling and releasing me. "But alas I am a patient man. Let's go see what Derek found."

I collect my clothes from last night, and rather than putting them on and trudging through the castle, I have a better idea. "I'm going to dematerialize, so don't be alarmed."

"I've wanted to see this," he admits.

Still naked with an arm full of clothes, I close my eyes and imagine my bathroom.

And just like that, I'm there.

Damn, I love this.

I shower the sex and the previous days romp through the cemetery off me and dress in a clean outfit, then meet the brothers in the dining room, where the children are finishing up breakfast.

Alina in Liam's arms with a milky bottle of blood,

Zara on the floor with her grilled shark, and Ana in a chair eating pancakes with syrup and blueberries.

"Yum, that looks good," I tell her.

She grins through syrupy lips. "It is!"

"I'll have what she's having," I announce to whatever ghosts are listening, but it's Matilda herself that comes out carrying more freshly made pancakes.

"Thank you," I say, accepting my plate. " I feel like we haven't spent much time together recently," I tell her as she sits next to Ana across from me.

"It is a strange time," she says ominously. "Join me for tea when you have a moment. Let us catch up."

"I will," I promise. With this ticking time bomb over my head, I'm becoming more aware of how precious these relationships are and how important it is to make time for the people I love, no matter what else is going on.

"What are you kids up to today?" Matilda asks.

"Research," Elijah says, sharing a meaningful glance with me.

"I'm going to try to get into the Ancient Library," I say. "Have you heard of it?"

Matilda's eyes widen, and then Alina begins crying and Zara joins her.

"Oh my," Matilda says, standing. "Let me take the babies upstairs so you kids can have your meeting."

Ana finishes up her last pancake and helps by picking up Zara, who clings to her. The five of them head upstairs, leaving me with the Night brothers.

Derek has been pacing, waiting until the kids were gone to speak.

"What did you find?" I finally ask, once we are completely alone.

"This," he says, holding out a Memory Catcher.

My heart nearly stops in my chest. "What does it show?" I ask.

"The murder," he says.

"Holy shit. How?"

He runs a hand through his hair, and I realize how disheveled he appears. He normally looks like he just stepped off the cover of GQ but this morning his hair is a mess, he's got a day old stubble covering his chin and his clothes are dusty and torn in places.

"I've been up all night hunting," he says. "Looking for animals that might have seen what happened. I must have caught the memories of every wildlife in the area until it occurred to me to try the fish in the pond where she was found."

He looks exasperated with himself for not thinking of that one sooner, and I let our water magic connect, giving him a little boost of love and confidence. His gaze lands on mine and he grins just a little as acknowledgement.

"Don't keep us in suspense, brother. Who killed her? If it was Dath'Racul I'll ring his neck myself," Liam says.

Derek frowns. "It wasn't the Fire Dragon."

He lays the crystal down and activates it.

I hold my breath as the holographic image starts to play and we see Lyx standing near the pool of water talking to someone, though we can't see who it is.

She looks happy. Excited. Probably about the work that's being done for her people. We were just about to move some families into their new homes that day.

Then there's a blur.

Lyx screams.

And a monstrous creature appears, reflected oddly through the water. It's golden and black, with malformed wings, a body covered in boils, a head that is misshapen with eyes too small and too wide apart, and a mouth too big. But what stands out the most is the protrusion coming from the side of its head. It's the exact size and shape of a unicorn horn, though it doesn't much resemble one in color and form.

The creatures wings expand and it crashes into Lyx, impaling her with its horn and shoving her into the water, where she falls.

Then the memory ends.

"The fish swam away when Lyx fell into the lake."

We all sit in stunned silence. "So, Racul is wrong, it wasn't his mother. It wasn't any of the dragons. But... what *is* that creature?" I look around the table hoping one of the brothers can shed some light on this.

Derek shrugs. "I've never seen or heard about anything like this in my life."

Well, shit. That's not good. "Elijah?"

"I've never come across anything like it in life or in

my books. It's... a bit curious. We have lived in both worlds for many lifetimes and represented and come across many beings of all kinds. It seems unlikely there would be one we have never at least heard of." He hesitates a moment before saying, "perhaps you can find something about it in the Ancient Library, if you're able to get in."

"Can I take that with me to show Racul?" I ask Derek.

None of them look thrilled at the idea but I persist. "He's a dragon. He might know something you don't. At the very least, it will show him it wasn't his mother. And if that's true, then maybe I don't have to find a way of fighting and defeating the Mother of Dragons in order to save this world."

"That is the good news," Sebastian agrees. "But Elijah, you should continue to research just in case. I still don't trust her. And if we have to go up against her, we need to be prepared."

"Agreed," Elijah says.

There's a knock at the door, and I stand. "I think my ride is here. Wish me luck."

I can tell none of them want to let me go, but we all know I have no choice.

Racul greets me when I open the door. "Have I arrived too early?" he asks.

"Nope. I'm ready to roll," I say, closing the door behind me. "How far is this place?" I ask as I look around for his carriage, but none is in sight.

"Too far for horses. You will ride me," he says, shifting into dragon form.

"Yeah, um, as tempting as that offer is," I say trying not to laugh. "I can actually fly, so let's try that first?"

"You think you can keep up with a dragon?" he scoffs, his voice even deeper now.

"Why don't we do this thing and find out?"

"Very well, Fate. But I'll be here when you tire."

Oof, the arrogance.

Racul takes off into the sky and I summon my magic to follow him.

He continues to accelerate, pushing his speed faster and faster. I'm pretty sure he's just trying to show off, but he doesn't know who he's messing with. I wrap air around me, using fire to stay warm, using light and darkness to give me an extra edge, and I keep pace side by side with him. I even give him a thumb's up when he glances my way, an incredulous look on his dragon face.

We fly like this for some time, and I do start to tire out, but I can't give him the satisfaction of knowing, so I push harder, determined that he and I will arrive together, as equals, and he can shut his mouth about it all. We are heading west and soon begin to pass over areas I've never been, though I recall these parts from the maps I studied in Elijah's office. Somewhere around here is giant territory, though I see no evidence of them at present.

And then we reach a place that doesn't exist on any

maps I've seen. A body of water that spans miles, with an isolated island stuck in the center. That appears to be our destination.

When he finally begins his descent, I'm so relieved I nearly cry, but I land like a boss and grin like it was nothing.

He shifts back into human form, and I pretend like I'm not completely exhausted.

"I was not expecting that," he says, a curious look on his face.

I'm pretty sure he keeps seeing his dead girlfriend in me, which is a bit creepy but also super sad, so I give him a pass and instead ask, "Where now?"

We are in a dense jungle in the middle of an island that looks like it shouldn't exist. The temperature is sweltering so I use my air magic to cool myself. Vines coil around tall trees and fall from thick branches like snakes waiting to snap. The dense undergrowth is teeming with a hidden world of insects. A canopy of lush foliage blocks out the view of the sky, and in the distance a strange kind of shriek that might be a monkey calls out.

Racul points west and I can see through the trees the ruins of an old castle that looks like nothing more than crumbled stone at this point. I follow the Fire Dragon to a spot in the center, stepping over heavy roots that have taken over the area, my boots sinking into the decomposing plant life of the jungle.

He points to an area thick with vines and undergrowth. "There should be a door here that only you and my mother can open."

I nod and use my earth magic to clear everything away, revealing a circular metal door with a handprint in the center. I place my hand on it, but nothing happens.

"Um, do you know what I'm supposed to do?" I ask.

"I've never actually seen it opened," he says. "Though I have tried myself."

Shit.

First, I go with Liam's approach to life. I try to blow shit up.

The fire ball lands on the metal door and fizzes out, having zero effect.

"I'm not impressed," Racul says, dryly.

"Good thing I'm not actually trying to impress you," I say.

Next I use my air and water magic it to create lightning that I zap from my hands, but again, nothing.

"This is getting us nowhere," the impatient dragon says.

I step aside and gesture to the door. "Would you like to try?"

He glares at me but says nothing.

"I didn't think so."

I kneel down again, studying the handprint. "Maybe if I channel my power into this?" I say, thinking out loud.

Pressing my hand against the cold metal, I rotate

through my elemental powers, but none of them work, and I'm getting a headache.

"This was a long trip for nothing," Racul says under his breath.

"You can shut it now," I say, pinching the bridge of my nose. There's one thing I still haven't tried.

Closing my eyes, I channel all six elements at once into the door, and finally I'm rewarded with a series of clicks and the sound of grinding as the cool metal beneath my palm falls away, revealing a long ladder into a dark hole.

"About time," Racul says.

I scowl at him. "How long did it take you to get in?"

He doesn't respond to that, but instead peers down into the darkness. "Ladies first," he says.

"Age before beauty," I say, and he frowns, but begins the decent.

I'm not ashamed to say that if there's a trap in there, I'd rather let him deal with it first.

"All clear, you can come down now," he shouts from below.

I descend quickly, cheating with some magic. It's dark and dank and I wonder how any books survived in these conditions. I hold out my palm and produce an orb of light to guide us through the tunnel. I have no idea if dragons can see in the dark, but it doesn't seem to be one of my superpowers.

We arrive at another door at the end of the long hallway, and it has another handprint on it. I sigh at the excessiveness of it all and use my palm and magic to open it.

It's pitch black within, so I shoot hundreds of orbs of light into the room to illuminate our way, and we both gasp at the same time at what we see.

The library is huge, and was clearly lined with thousands of books and scrolls. But it's been ransacked. If I didn't know better, I'd say tomb raiders have been here.

Everything is torn apart and all the books and whatever artifacts may have been preserved in the glass cabinets are gone.

Racul walks in, his eyes wide. "Who could have done this?"

"Logically, if only the Fates and your mother could gain access, and the Fates have been gone for thousands of years... then..."

His face is grim at the thought. "She did this to cover her crimes."

Oh right. "Speaking of, I meant to tell you. I have a Memory Catcher of Lyx's death. It wasn't your mother."

"Show me," he says.

I pull it out and play it for him. He watches silently and when it's over he just shakes his head. "I still believe she is behind it. Somehow. Maybe she is controlling the creature?" he asks.

"Or maybe she didn't do it, and we need to be

looking at this differently. Do you know what manner of being this is?" I ask.

He shakes his head. "I have never seen something like that in my life. It appears to have traits of a dragon and maybe a unicorn, but that does not make sense. Our species cannot interbreed. It is impossible. Besides that, it is clearly the product of some great evil, which neither dragons or unicorns are."

His logic seems a little self-serving and flawed, but I can't deny this creature seems to defy the natural order according to everyone who knows about such things.

"Let's look around," I say, disappointment flooding me as I realize I'd hung all my hopes on finding answers here, and now they were as useful as dead butterflies pinned to a cork board for display. Still, I hold onto what optimism I can summon. "Maybe we will find something."

He looks as doubtful as I feel. The place, after all, has been well and truly ransacked, but still we begin sorting through the scarps that remain.

There are a few books left, but they offer nothing useful. I'm not sure why they were kept here at all, to be honest. *A History of Cheese in Northern Europe*, for example, which looks brought over from my world. Like, okay, thanks. That's super-secret shit to save in an underground Ancient Library. Still, I add it to my bag in case Elijah finds it interesting.

I spend another hour scouring every inch of the

place, and in a dusty corner under a thick coating of cobwebs I discover a trunk that looks promising. " Racul, check it out."

He saunters over, his face reflecting my own lack of success. But something in this chest feels important. My magic is tingling in my fingertips, and I use that power to unlock the trunk and open it.

The only thing inside is a deep velvet purple cloak with silver trim and embroidery, and a mother of pearl clasp that holds it at the neck.

I pull it out, shaking off the dust, and hold it up.

Racul 's eyes narrow. "I recognize that," he says. "It belonged to the Maiden Fate."

Me.

This was mine?

Or my past selves at any rate.

I drape it over my shoulders and I am thrown into a memory that feels so vivid, it's as if I could be living it right now.

I STAND NEXT to my sisters. They are not sisters by blood, I know this, but by power, by destiny, by Fate. We are the Fates and we are draped in our royal robes. I wear purple, the Crone wears emerald green, and the Mother wears sapphire blue. We have silver masks that cover our faces, allowing us to keep our mystery, and we stand before the Mother of Dragons, who is angry, but I do not remember why.

We turn to leave, and once we are alone, the Mother takes off her mask, and I see the beautiful face of Landal, her blue eyes that match her robes glistening with tears. "We have made a grave mistake in what we have done," she says.

The Crone nods. "It is as you say. We should never have agreed to this."

I take off my mask and see in a mirror my own face, similar to what it is now.

And then the Crone removes her mask, and my present self gasps as I collapse to my knees.

The face unveiled before me is one I know.

One I trust.

I am looking at the face of Matilda Night.

THE MONSTER

"We delight in the beauty of the butterfly, but rarely admit the changes it has gone through to achieve that beauty."
   ~Maya Angelou

RACUL INSISTS on returning with me to the castle, though I'm not sure his presence will make this conversation go easier. Since time is of the essence, and I need to know what the hell is going on, I suggest teleporting us both.

"I prefer to fly," he says.

"That's fine. But I'm not going to wait for you, though."

He pauses, clearly torn between wanting to be a part of the conversation, and not wanting to trust me with dematerializing him.

"Clocks ticking, buddy. I'm leaving now." I have the cloak—my cloak—stuck in my bag. Touching it, holding it, feels like connecting with a part of myself I'm still trying to find.

And Matilda must have known this whole time who, and what, I was. Why didn't she tell me? Why didn't she help me? Why has she kept her identity a secret?

Racul cocks his head, studying me. "You feel betrayed. But you must know, the Fates identities were never revealed to anyone. Not even my mother knew who they were. Nor did the Druids. Their secrets are what kept them safe."

"Except I am a Fate. She knew that. She could have told me." I pause. "And besides, Landal told you, didn't she?"

He glances away. "And that trust ended her life."

My own feelings give way to compassion as I see the hurt he carries with him. He's a giant ass. He has been since I've known him. But he's also someone in pain, like all of us. Someone who lost a person he loved. I can relate to that. My brother's death still tears at the fabric of my soul on a daily basis, though it's getting easier to bear, if easier is the right word.

I take a step closer to him. "You don't know that for sure," I say. "And even if it's true, I believe she would still make the same choice, to share the life she had with you while she could. I don't remember much of my time as a Fate, but I do know that life is never guaranteed, even for immortals. And spending your life hiding behind a mask is no way to live. She had love. She gave love. That's a lot for any life," I say. "Really, that's everything."

He sucks in a breath. "Take me with you," he says. "Just try not to kill us both."

I grin. "I'll do my best, but no promises."

I take his hand and close my eyes, this time avoiding the gardens and instead imagining the open area in front of the house. In a flash, we arrive, and Racul staggers as we land. I steady him and smile at the fact that I didn't send us anywhere too terrible.

"That was... awful," he says. "

"It was rough my first time too," I say. "You get used to it."

"I will not be doing this again to get used to it," he says in a clipped bass voice.

We walk into the castle and find Liam first. The dragon and the Druid stare each other down, heat building in the room and their bodies sizzling with fire.

"Settle down boys. Bigger fish to fry right now." I turn to Liam. "Where's Matilda? And where's everyone else?"

Liam doesn't stop staring Racul down as he answers me. "My brothers are around here somewhere. Lily and Kaya are at the grove. The babies are napping, and Matilda is upstairs with Ana. Why? What's wrong?"

I don't answer, I just head straight to Matilda's

room, my heart and head at war for how to approach the woman I have come to love like a grandmother.

Along the way, we seem to collect the remaining brothers, who are all wondering what's going on and why we have one of the dragon's in our house.

Matilda sits in her rocking chair in front of the fire, a cup of tea at her side. Green beads woven into her gray hair. Her eyes heavy and dark. Ana is napping with a new doll Lily made her in the corner on a mat. As soon as Matilda sees my face, she knows.

She stands and gestures for us to leave so we don't disturb Ana's nap.

"The girl hasn't been sleeping well," Matilda says. "She has night terrors every evening. She can only seem to get any rest during the day."

We walk down the hall into a sitting room that's seldom used. It has a large glass door that leads to a spacious balcony overlooking one of the gardens with overstuffed chairs and couches that are arranged for conversation in the center of the room, and a fireplace in the corner to ward off the chill that all castles inherently have. Thick rugs cover the stone floor and tapestries of gardens hang on the walls. Matilda and I sit across from each other. Liam and Sebastian sit on either side of me, Elijah takes a chair by the fire, and Derek and Racul flank Matilda on the other couch. It's an incongruous group, and we are awkward with each other.

"Why?" I ask. "Why didn't you tell me?"

The Night brothers look to each other in silent question, then to me to find out what I'm talking about. My relationship with their grandmother has always been affectionate, loving, close. They've never seen me upset with her.

Matilda sighs sadly. "I wanted to. Many times. I tried. But I have spent thousands of years keeping my identity a secret. And when I saw you, when you responded to the ad, I just couldn't believe it. At first, I thought it must be an unlikely coincidence. What were the odds that the Maiden Fate would return in the human world, so unprepared for her own life and powers? Then your magic began to manifest, and I couldn't deny the truth, but I convinced myself it would be better for you not to know."

"I'm confused," Liam says, looking between the two of us.

"That seems a common state for you," Racul says snidely.

I glare at the dragon and then look to Liam, waiting to see if Matilda will fill him in.

"My boys, there is something I have been keeping from you four for many years." She pauses, the truth clearly so hard to say, even now. "I am the Crone Fate."

Her words land like a live bomb in the room, and no one speaks, so she continues.

"When my sisters died, I went into hiding and gave up my role as Fate, instead, committing to my life as Matilda alone."

Liam sits stone faced, his emotions burning deep within him. I can feel the flare of his fire, his anger, pain, confusion. The tether between us lights up with it, and I send along a soothing stream of water and air magic to calm him.

Sebastian is stoic, as always, pushing his feelings down deep. Elijah is curious but I feel the strain of hurt underneath, and Derek is awash in deep and roiling emotion that he's barely holding onto.

But I understand their feelings. I haven't known Matilda nearly as long as they have, their betrayal must feel much greater. Especially given all the shit that went down with the Fates. I know my past self-role in their lives wasn't stellar. I made Cole's brothers torture and punish him. Or she did. It's so hard to see that person as myself, when she did things I couldn't imagine ever doing.

And why didn't Matilda stop that from happening? What role did she have in all that?

I feel even worse as I recall their story of being banished from the Order and destroyed with the Unforgivable Curse. They never said who cast the curse, but it must have been the Fates. That would make the most sense. Does that mean Matilda and I were responsible for their descent into madness? For their destruction of villages, animals, and lives?

A wave of nausea overtakes me and I sit forward, my head pulsing with heat and pain. A flash hits me but I can't quite grasp it. I'm too overwhelmed by grief for the karmic pain I've wrought.

Liam puts a hand on my back. "Are you sick?"

I look up at him, my eyes filled with tears. "I am so sorry for what we did to you back then."

He frowns. "That wasn't you. Not really." He looks over to Matilda. "But it *was* you. *You* are still the same person you were. You didn't stop the Mother Fate when she cursed us. You didn't stop the Maiden when she made us punish our own brother. You knew us. And you didn't protect us."

The other three brothers are silent, letting Liam speak their rage for them.

Tears fill the old woman's eyes. "I should have done more. I did what I could behind the scenes. It wasn't enough, but I tried. I was one voice amongst three and towards the end we didn't agree on a lot. Landal—the Mother—she wanted to kill Cole for what he did. And she wanted to kill all of you when you rebelled. When you stopped doing what you were told."

"Death would have been a kindness compared to what was done to us," he says, the fire leaving him as sadness takes its place. "We destroyed so many lives because of that curse."

"I know, my boy," Matilda says. "I know. And I cannot be more sorry for my role in all of it. But I couldn't let any of you die. I loved you all too much."

I glance at Racul and his face is impassive. Hard. I

wonder what he knew about Landal's role in all of this. Or if he even cares about any of this.

I take Liam's hand in mine, holding it tight, letting him know he's not alone. Not anymore. Not ever again.

As reluctant as I am to change the focus of this conversation, I know I must. We haven't a lot of time. "Matilda, I had a vision when I was at the library. The three Fates were together after a confrontation with the Mother of Dragons. It seemed we all regretted something we'd done. What did we do?"

Matilda gasps and puts her hand to her mouth. "We can never speak of that. It doesn't matter. It was destroyed."

"What was?" I ask.

"The abomination we helped create."

A sinking feeling fills my gut and I pull the Memory Catcher out of my pocket and play the memory for Matilda. When it comes to the creature that killed Lyx, I pause it. "Was that what we made?"

Matilda's eyes widen. "It's not possible. It was destroyed. The Mother of Dragons knew what she'd done was wrong. She..."

"This is what killed Lyx." I say. "You must tell me the truth. What is this creature?"

Gods, if only I could remember myself.

"It's time you knew everything," she says. "The Mother of Dragons was in love with the Queen of the Unicorns. They wanted a child together, but their races could not mate, nor could two females. So, they petitioned the Fates to help them merge their magic into a child."

I could see my own emotions reflected on the faces of the others. None of them knew about this, though Racul certainly suspected his mother had been up to shady shit. But this? Gods be damned, how stupid could they all be? That was clearly a recipe for poison cookies right there. And I was a part of this? I was a moron.

"So that clearly didn't go well," I say.

"No, it didn't." She rubs her eyes. "What we made... well, you've seen. It was... monstrous."

"And my mother killed it?" Racul asks.

"Yes," Matilda says. "Or so we thought."

Pain lances through my brain and I grip Liam's hand tighter as a Flash rushes through me. "Something is coming," I whisper through gritted teeth, but before anyone can do anything about it, the door to our room explodes in shards of splintered wood and the most hideous creature I've ever seen bursts in, sharp teeth dripping with saliva, yellow eyes crazed.

It's so much worse in person than in the memory, I realize.

Matilda stands and pulls out a wand from her robes, channeling her magic through it to blast the monster with an electric bolt.

It absorbs the impact of the attack and seems to grow stronger from it. The horn on the side of its head spins like a drill, and its wings extend, propelling it through the room. I'm still too sick to be of much help, my brain feeling as if it will explode.

Liam hits it with a blaze of fire, but once again, the attack has no impact other than seeming to make it stronger and faster. It now crackles with lightning and burns with the fire of the Druid.

Derek tries to drive it away with wind, but it uses its wings to push through.

Lovely.

Matilda shouts at the monster. "Be gone you beast, you abomination. Be gone!" Once again, she uses her wand to attack, but this time the bolt of lightning is directed back at her and she's hit in the chest and collapses to the floor.

Ignoring my pounding head, I run to her, nearly vomiting at the movement.

I can't tell if she's alive or not. "Liam! Help her!"

Despite his own anger, he comes to her and checks her pulse, but the monster descends on us, and I am in the direct line of its fire. I attempt to create a shield to protect us, but I'm not fast enough.

Just as the monster is about to impale me with its drill horn, Racul jumps in between us and the horn plunges into him instead. He's hit with such force that both he and the creature crash through the glass window, over the balcony and into the garden.

The light rain that had begun earlier is now a raging storm, darkening the Dragon's Breath in the sky and turning everything murky and wet.

With fear pulsing through my veins, I plunge into my power and pull on every strand I can find, then fly through the broken glass and down to where Racul and the monster are.

Racul lays unconscious in a bush as rain pelts him.

The monster turns to me, and using all the elements, I weave a cocoon trap that I throw on it. This seems to work for a moment, as a magical net wraps around the beast and slows its progression.

But it breaks free too soon and lunges at me.

In a blink, the four Night brothers jump off the balcony with ease and join me.

I grab the hands of the two nearest brothers while they form a circle around the monster, hands held. I channel the power they offer in addition to my own and cast another shield around the creature, this time creating a dome prison in which to trap it.

The monster screams and thrashes against the barrier but the power I've thrown into the barrier zaps it back each time it hits.

"I think it's holding," I say, my body buzzing and my head pounding.

I feel as if I'm about to vomit.

I sag into Sebastian's arms and he catches me, holding me close.

"Matilda?" I ask.

"She's alive," Liam says.

"Racul!" I scream and pull out of Sebastian's arms and run over to the Fire Dragon. His body is crumbled in a bush and I tug at him to turn him over. There's a horn sized hole in his chest and he's not breathing.

"Liam?" I ask, knowing he won't love helping but he's a healer before anything.

True to form he rushes over and examines the dragon. There's no gloat in his face when he turns to me and frowns. "He's dead."

THE TRUTH

"Look for the answer inside your question."
  ~Rumi

THE STORM CONTINUES to rage around us and a deep dread builds within me. I stare at Racul's body and can't stop shaking. He died to save me, which goes against everything I thought I knew about the Fire Dragon.

His burnt red skin looks paler in death, as if the flames of his soul are being extinguished. I take his hand, but it is heavy and limp. A tear slides down my cheek. I didn't exactly like the man, but over the last few days I had developed a kind of bond with him, and this death hurts. They all hurt.

I turn to look at the creature in the makeshift cage

we created. Its thrashing has calmed, and it seems to be tiring out.

In fact, it looks to be curling up to rest. The fight must have drained it.

As it falls asleep, we all watch in stunned silence as its body begins to glow and its shape changes. Its legs lengthen, its body shortens, its head becomes smaller, until it's no longer a hideous monster at all.

It's a girl.

A girl we all know.

It's Ana.

I place Racul's hand on his chest and walk over to look more closely.

Ana sleeps fitfully, crying out until she wakes herself with her own terrors. When she sees where she is, she screams and cries. "Please let me out, I'm scared."

I kneel to speak to her. "Ana, do you know why you're here?" I ask.

She shakes her head. "I'm scared."

"You turned into something else," I say, unsure of how to phrase this. "Do you remember that?"

"No. I don't know what you mean?"

"You attacked us," I say softly. Nothing about this feels right, and I don't know how to process what's happening. My flash is buzzing madly.

Her eyes widen and she begins to cry. "I didn't. I promise. It wasn't me."

She's either the world's best actress or she really doesn't remember doing it.

"What's the last thing you remember?" I ask.

"I was sleeping in Grandmother Matilda's room and I heard someone calling me. I opened my eyes, felt a pain, and then I was here."

"You remember nothing else? Nothing at all?" Sebastian asks, kneeling next to me.

"No. What happened? What do you think I did?"

Shit. How do you tell a small child she's a killer?

I look over at Sebastian, whose jaw is locked. He shrugs, but doesn't take his eyes off Ana.

Ana looks past us, her eyes widening when she sees Racul in the bushes. "Why is he like that?" she asks, breaking into sobs again.

I want to reach through the barrier and hold her. She's so small and scared and I just don't believe she's done this on purpose. But the fact is, she did do it, and I can't risk letting her free to do it again.

"Is he dead?" she asks. "Why is he like that?" She's screaming and shaking, and I can't leave her alone like this.

Against my better judgement, I move through the barrier and into the space with her. Sebastian shouts for me to stop, but I can't let this poor little girl suffer alone.

She clings to me, sobbing into my shoulder, her frail arms wrapped around me. "Tell me what's happening? Why do people keep dying?"

"I don't know what's going on, honey. But we're

going to figure it out. Until then, you're going to have to stay in here. For your own safety."

She looks up, eyes wide. "No. You can't leave me in here alone. No! I'm scared."

It's a terrible place to leave a child, but she's not just a child. She's a creation gone wrong. And where has she been all this time? What brought her back if the Fate's were so certain she was killed?

"I'll make it nicer for you," I say. "Watch."

I don't need to be touching the Nights to do this anymore. Instead, I place my hand in the earth and request help from the flowers surrounding us. I telegraph the image of what I want to do, and they agree.

My magic is connected to the brothers through our new bond, and I tap into that to help. As my power flows, a small room forms around me and Ana, made of beautiful flowers and vines and leaves. It's tall enough for her to stand and walk around, and mounds of mossy grass make up a bed and small couch.

She looks around, her fear momentarily forgotten as she watches in awe at the earth reforming itself for her.

When I'm done, I feel exhausted, but she smiles. Then her mouth drops when she realizes she has to stay here. "Please don't leave me," she begs.

"I'm so sorry honey, I have to. But I'll send out your doll, and I'll come visit you often while we figure out what to do, okay?"

She sobs softly as I leave.

The other brothers have gone upstairs to check on Matilda, but Sebastian stayed behind to wait for me. He takes my hand as I leave the barrier. "That was risky," he says, as we walk back to the house.

"I know. But I couldn't just leave her."

"I know," he says softly, squeezing my hand.

I glance back at Racul 's body and my heart lurches. "What do we do about him?" I ask.

"We'll send for Ifi and Elal. But we will have to explain this somehow. We have to turn the girl over to the Mother of Dragons."

I pull back from him. "We can't. She didn't mean to do this. We have to figure out what's going on."

We enter the house and Elijah is coming downstairs, his face distraught. "What's wrong?" I ask, releasing Sebastian's hand to rush over to him.

"Matilda is unconscious and can't be woken. Liam doesn't know why. She's alive, but appears to be in a coma. We've put her in her room for now and Liam is working on potions. I'm heading to my office to look for a book that might help."

Oh gods, this is awful.

I want to check on Matilda, but I know my presence won't help anything, so instead I retrieve Ana's doll with some food and water and take it to her, then join Sebastian in the family library. He's staring into the fire as I take a seat next to him.

"How was she?" he asks.

"She'd already fallen back to sleep. Poor kid."

"You don't know for sure that she's innocent of intent," he says. "If she's doing this deliberately, then she could be very skilled at lying. She was created a long time ago. She's not an ordinary child. She might not be a child at all."

My stomach turns at that. I hadn't considered the possibility that her entire presentation was a lie. Still. "I felt something from her. A connection to her magic. It doesn't feel evil to me. With my darkness and light, I could suss out intention better than most, and hers feels pure. She's genuinely scared. Maybe she just needs to learn control."

"And yet she's only killed dragons," he says. "And not all dragons. She didn't harm Zara. That doesn't feel random or lacking control to me."

Liam, Elijah and Derek join us downstairs, Liam carrying Alina and Derek carrying the baby dragon.

They put the babies in the crib and take seats in front of the fire with us.

"Any news?" I ask Liam.

"It's a waiting game now," he says.

Derek stands and begins pacing, his trademark go to for stressful times and thinking. "At least now we can resolve these murders and save the Otherworld," he says. "When we turn over the monster, Amora should honor her word and leave us alone."

Oh boy. "We're not turning over the child," I say.

They all look at me with unreadable expressions.

So I make the same argument I just made to Sebastian. "I felt it in her. She doesn't know what she's doing, but from what I've seen of the Mother of Dragons, she won't care. In fact, she's the reason we're in this mess to begin with. She created this child and tried to destroy her. Now the child is back."

And the timing is awfully... coincidental.

"Callia!" I shout. "Show yourself!"

The unicorn always turns up when she feels like it. I've never been able to summon her, but she has to know what's going on.

"Callia!"

Finally, the unicorn appears before me, her face grim. I glare at her. "Did you know all along?"

She shakes her head. "I didn't. Not at first."

"So it's true? This is the child which the Queen of the Unicorns and the Mother of Dragons created together?"

Her head drops. "It is. She is. And I loved her with all my heart. I did not want to destroy her, even though she wasn't what we expected."

"We?" I ask, the puzzle pieces in my mind suddenly rearranging themselves once again.

Her large silver eyes gloss over. "I am... was... the queen of my people. My relationship with Amora was... unexpected. We were enemies but we fell in love. We thought a child together could bridge the gap between our kind."

"Then why did you let Amora kill her?"

She looks up at me, her expression filled with complex emotion. "I didn't let her. I told her she would have to kill me first. So, she did."

I gasp and tell the brothers what Callia just told me. It would be a lot easier if everyone could see the damn unicorn.

"Do you know what happened after?" I ask. "To your child?"

I can tell she does. She sighs and gazes into the distance, into a past so far gone it's hard for me to imagine. "As I died, I used the last of my power to create a small slice of a new world, and I pulled my dying child into it and left her there. I thought it would be better, for her to live, but I was wrong."

And then it all clicks. "When Ava'Kara and I expanded the world, we pulled her into it, didn't we? That's why she's back?"

Callia nods. "I do believe that's what happened, yes."

My stomach sinks with the unintended consequences of my actions. "Why is she targeting and killing the dragons?" I ask.

"That I do not know. But she is innocent, you have seen that yourself. Please do not sacrifice her to Amora's ambitions."

A tear slides down Callia's cheek. "I'm going to see my daughter now," she says, and blinks out.

I face the Night brothers, prepared to fight for this girl's life. She's already been tormented too much.

"We cannot harbor a serial killer," Derek says. "She puts all of us—this entire world—at risk. She was never meant to exist at all," he argues. "We must let her go. It's the only way."

I expect Liam to side with Derek, but he surprises me. "No. I'm with Eve on this. If there's a chance she's innocent of intent, we must find another way. We have spent lifetimes defending the guilty, making sure they get a fair trial. We cannot turn this child over to someone we know will torture and destroy her. That's not who we are."

Elijah cocks his head, taking in all the information. "I think we should hold off making any decisions until we know more. I can't deny turning her over would be the most expedient solution to our problems, but I also do not feel it wise to turn our back on our own values for sake of the convenient solution. That is not who we are, nor is it who we have ever been."

Sebastian shakes his head. "I'm sympathetic, I am. But... " he glances at me and I know what he's about to do.

"Don't," I say.

"I'm sorry," he says. "But they have to know. It's too important."

I close my eyes and know that in a moment, everything will shift, and it will be my fault.

"What do we need to know," Liam says, glancing at me.

I can't speak it, so Sebastian does.

"Eve is connected to this world," he says. "As a Fate, through the spell work she did to expand it. If the world is destroyed, she will die."

The room falls silent as they each process what this means.

Elijah speaks first. "This changes things," he says, turning sad eyes to me. "We cannot risk your life for this."

"My life is a small matter in the bigger scheme of things. Let's say we hand over Ana to her. Then what? She tortures and kills the child she created? Or who knows what? Are we sure she'll honor her agreement to spare the world? Racul didn't think so. And what happens next time she gets a wild hair up her ass? She comes at us again with different demands?" I ask, making eye contact with each of them. "No, we cannot allow her to hold this world hostage."

"What do you propose?" Elijah asks.

"I don't know," I admit. "But at least give me time to think about it before we ruin this child's life. There's a piece we're missing. I'm sure of it."

An urgent knock at the door interrupts us and when no one makes a move, I go to answer it.

I'm stunned to see the tall, stunning Earth Dragon

in human form standing there. Her skin is a deep ochre and her eyes are emerald green with touches of brown. Her wings are also flecked with the same green, and drape around her like a cloak. Her hair falls to her knees in thick waves of different shades of earthy brown mixed with the greens of a lush wilderness, with thin vines woven through tiny braids.

"Brock'Mir," I say, instinctively touching her ring on my hand. We met briefly of course, the day I got her ring, but we've never really spoken, and I certainly didn't expect her to show up at my front door.

"Maiden Fate," she says formally, her voice husky and full of earthy resonance. "You must come with me. To the Broken Cathedral. We have all felt the death of two more of my brothers." Her face is pained when she says this, and the reality of what is happening hits me harder than it did before.

In the chaos of the world ending and trying to solve the mystery, somehow, I lost sight of the fact that these immortal creatures are losing their family, their siblings, one by one. My brother's death is still raw in my heart, and on instinct I pull the dragon into my arms, though she towers over me. "I am so sorry," I say through thick emotions. "I have been through some fraction of the pain you are going through and I know it is hell."

She stiffens a moment, then relents and returns the affection of the hug briefly, before pulling away. Her eyes glisten with emotion but it is quickly wiped way by her pragmatism.

"Thank you, Eve," she says. "But I'm afraid there is no time for mourning right now. My mother has arrived, and she is threatening to destroy the world now, not in the timeframe she originally promised. You must come and help me stop her, or everyone in the Otherworld will die tonight."

THE CAVE

So close that your hand on my chest is my hand,
So close that your eyes close as I fall asleep
~Pablo Neruda, Sonnet XVII

SHIT. Double and triple shit.

I rush back into the house to explain to the guys where I'm going.

"We're going with you," Sebastian says, standing.

"I'll be fine," I say. "Besides, Racul's body needs to be handled, the babies need to be watched, someone needs to keep an eye on Ana, and we can't leave Matilda alone. Also, someone needs to get word to Lily about what happened. She's probably at the grove with Kaya."

"I'll send a note out to let Lily know what

happened, and I'll send a runner to fetch Ifi and Elal to handle the body," Elijah says.

"I'll keep an eye on Matilda," Liam says. "And take care of the babies."

Derek looks over. "I can make sure the dome holds for Ana until we figure out what to do."

"So everything is handled," Sebastian says. "Which means I'm coming with you."

I'm about to argue when Liam interrupts. "You're going to face off with the most powerful being in the world, who wants to destroy everything today," Liam says, his face stoic. "You should take at least one of us for the extra power."

"I know, but like I said, I'll be fine." I grin but he's not buying it, and my grin drops. "Look, I won't lie. I'm nervous as hell, but we don't have time to argue. I've got to go now."

As if on cue, my head splits and I double over in pain. Sebastian catches me in his arms before I fall to the ground. "What happened?" he asks, concern written all over his face.

"She's starting to tear the world apart. I have to go now!"

"You can't go alone like this," Sebastian says, sending earth magic to steady me through our bond.

When I can stand, I nod reluctantly. "Fine, let's go," I say. We rush back to Brock and I grab her hand. "He's coming with us," I say to the dragon, who looks skeptical but there's no time to argue. "Ready?"

She nods, and I focus. I've never done this with two people before, but how much harder can it be?

Ha! Famous last words.

I feel like I've contracted food poisoning as I dematerialize us and travel to the Broken Cathedral. Waves of nausea crash through me but I somehow manage to avoid vomiting into the void. Amora and the Darkness Dragon are arguing when we land on top of the Cathedral, in the same spot where I killed Jerry—or he killed himself through me—and I break out into a sweat at the memory, which doesn't help the nausea one bit.

Amora is in her dragon form, hovering over us and casting a giant shadow over everything. Golden light blazes forth from her mouth as she screams out her pain into the world, shaking its very foundation. The storm we've been dealing with all day rages uncontrollably around us.

My hair whips in the wind, cutting into my face as it does. I'm soaked to the bone despite my fire magic blazing within me to keep me warm. Lightning flashes in the sky, splitting a tree on the ground near us. It catches flames but is put out by the rain.

"Stop!" I scream, channeling my Fate powers until I'm glowing with them. I ride a wind current and rise above the building to face her. "You cannot do this. Not now! Not yet."

"More of my children are dead," she screams, her eyes glowing with fury, her voice layered with power that nearly undoes me.

"And so you would murder even more innocent people?" I shout. "You gave your word. Does that mean nothing?"

"This world does not deserve to live!" As she screams, thunder crashes through the Dragon's Breath, shaking the ground.

"This is our world," Brock says, transforming into her dragon form and rising up with us. "You cannot take it from us."

Ra'Terr takes longer to join, and when he does arrive, his deep ebony black looks greyed out and he appears less vibrant than he was.

Sebastian remains on the roof watching from below. But I can feel him sending me as much power as he can, and I'm glad he came with me.

This is all terrifying, but I put on a brave face against the Mother—and Queen— of the Dragons.

"You are my children," the queen says. "I must do this to protect you."

"You are taking from them a piece of them," I say. "What do you think it will do to your remaining children if you destroy the world they helped build? A part of them will die too."

She pauses at that, looking at the two dragons flanking her. "I should never have let you do this thing," she says. "If we had stayed in our world, all would be well. Dath'Racul would rule by my side. You would all have your own kingdoms. Our world would be at peace. This world would never exist."

"If we had stayed in our world," Brock says, "we would have let all these people die. They cannot survive in the mortal world any longer. The humans have taken over and made it inhospitable for anyone else. And we are the reason these people exist."

My ears perk at that. This is the first time I've heard that particular news.

"What does that mean?" I ask.

Brock looks at me. "Magic exists because of dragons. When our kind began breeding with human, mixing our blood with them, it created all the races that now exist. These people are our people. These races exist because our kind fell in love with humans."

The queen rages again, spewing boiling golden lava from her mouth that destroys a side of the Cathedral. Sebastian has to dodge to avoid being hit himself.

Brock continues, now focused on her mother. "We owed it to them to create a world of safety for their kind."

"We owe these mixed bloods nothing," she sneers. "Dragons should have never shared their bloodline with such inferior beings."

Ha! That's rich coming from the woman who created a magical baby hybrid monster with her lover. But then, maybe that's part of the problem. She's punishing the world for her own mistakes.

"And yet they did," Brock says. "We cannot turn our back on our people." She pauses. "If you destroy the world now, I will not leave. I will die with it."

Ra'Terr nods his giant black dragon head. "As will I," he says.

"And your grandchild will also die," I say, pulling my last card. "We are still searching for her, but she's in this world somewhere. If you destroy it now, not only will you never find out who killed your children, but you will lose your last two children and your only grandchild."

I swallow a lump in my throat and pray to whatever gods are listening that she will be swayed by our words.

Finally, she lowers herself back to the roof, turning into her human form. The other dragons do as well, until we are all facing each other. Sebastian rushes to my side as support.

"I do not understand your loyalty to this wretched place," she says. "But I will honor my word. On one condition," she says, looking to her children. "When this is over, however it ends, you agree to come home with me and take your rightful places in our kingdom. Swear to it on the blood of the dragons."

I hold my breath, waiting.

Ra'Terr nods. "If we all make it through this, I will come home."

Brock hesitates, but eventually nods too. "Very well. I swear it on the blood of the dragons."

The queen doesn't look happy, despite getting her way. "I will hold you all to your promises." Then she turns her golden eyes to me. "You are running out of time, Fate. Bring me my children's killer and my grand-child, or be prepared to face the consequences."

Then she returns to her dragon form and flies high into the sky, her wings expanding to cover so much of the Dragon's Breath I can barely see anything beside her as she uses her magic to tear a hole in the fabric of this world and disappears.

I half expect the storm to stop the moment she's gone, but it continues to rage around us, and the Dark-ness Dragon slumps against his sister.

"Fate, before you leave, I must speak with you. Privately," he says, glancing at his sister who seems to know what this is about and nods.

Sebastian looks reluctant to let me go, but he waits with Brock as Ra'Terr and I walk to a corner of the Cathedral where there is a bit of shelter from the rain.

We both sit, our backs against a wall.

"There is something you should know," he says, his voice sounding weak.

"What is it?"

"I am dying," he says bluntly.

"What? How?" My mind tries to wrap itself around this news, but I am too stunned to make sense of it.

"In the darkness of my own cave, I was attacked." He pulls up his shirt to reveal a deep wound that is turning black at the edges. "Whatever did this to me, it left its poison in me and I will not last much longer."

"Did you see what attacked you?" I ask, my heart sinking with the answer I know is coming.

"A monstrous creature, though I only saw it for a moment."

Ana.

Gods. That means... The Mother of Dragons is going to lose her shit when she realizes Ra'Terr is dying too. There will only be one of her children left then.

And Brock'Mir will have to live the rest of her long life without her siblings. The truth of that crushes me.

I don't know The Darkness Dragon well at all. He is like a shadow, dark and mysterious. He keeps to himself. But I take his hand nonetheless, and let my dark magic flow into him, but I wrap it in light, because the two cannot exist without each other.

Cole taught me that.

His ebony eyes fill with tears, and I have a feeling this isn't a man who cries often. "I have not told anyone this, not even my sister, but since the attack... I have felt fear. It is the first time in my long life I have felt such a thing. The darkness used to be my haven, my element, and now I find myself scared of the dark." He chuckles, but it is a humorless sound of self-deprecation. "How silly is that? For a being of darkness to fear the dark?"

"None of us are made of just one thing," I say. "There is light in your darkness, just as there is darkness in light. Maybe it is time to step into the light, just a little. My father used to tell me *in lumen et lumen*. To be in the light and of the light."

His hand squeezes mine. "I have spent millennia in the dark. I do not know what to do with the light."

"I spent so much of my life fighting to live in the light, that when I found out I had darkness in me, I feared it," I confess. "Perhaps we all have to face the parts of us we fear and embrace them. This could be your time to do just that."

We sit there in silence a moment, then Ra'Terr stands, and I join him. "Thank you, Eve, Maiden Fate. You have brought me hope."

We walk back to Brock and Sebastian and Brock rushes to her brother. "I must get him home," she says, reaching for Ra'Terr. "Let us meet soon to discuss next steps." She pauses, looking at me carefully. "But before we go, I must say this. I know you have Ava'Zara, my sister's daughter."

I open my mouth to say... well, I'm not really sure what I'm going to say, but she holds up her free hand. "Wait. I understand why you took her. I believe you have a good heart, Eve Oliver. And you didn't know which amongst us you could trust. You were keeping her safe."

Relief floods me at her words.

"Are you going to take her away now that you know?"

She hesitates. "I want to. You are not equipped to raise a dragon. I do not know how you are even feeding her."

"Cooked shark is her favorite," I volunteer.

She raises an eyebrow. "Be that as it may, you are not wrong that she might be safer with you for now. As dragons are being killed off, we cannot be trusted to keep her safe. So take care of my niece, but when the time is right, I will bring her home."

My heart tugs at that. Ava'Zara has already become so close to Alina. The two of them are nearly inseparable. But Brock is right, we aren't in a position to raise a dragon. She will quickly outgrow our space and she needs her own kind to teach her their ways.

But that's a problem for another day.

"Take care of your brother. We will talk soon." She transforms and her brother climbs onto her back, looking weaker by the minute. But before she leaves, I add, "And come visit Zara when you'd like. She would enjoy that."

Brock nods and then takes off, soaring into the sky with Ra'Terr clutching her back.

Once they leave, Sebastian turns to me. "What was that about?"

I tell him what Ra'Terr shared.

"She's even more dangerous than we thought," Sebastian says, frowning. "We should get back to tell the others."

I nod and take a step toward Sebastian, but I stumble. I feel sick and weak and dizzy.

"You need to rest," he says.

I shake my head. "We need to get home, like you said."

I grip his hand and try to teleport us back to the castle. But even as we begin to disintegrate, I can feel it all going wrong. I'm too tired, too drained from all the magic I've been expending.

I screw up, and when we land, it is with a crash that results in bone deep pain that makes me almost pass out.

We look around to find a wilderness with mountains surrounding us. The storm is still raging on, so violently it's already pulled some trees from their roots.

Sebastian looks pale, but his stoicism holds him in good form, and he kneels at my side, examining me. "Is anything broken?" he asks, concern edging his voice.

I can barely hear him through the screams of the wind and the damage it's doing to the nature around us. "No. I don't think so. Just the wind knocked out of me," I say as loudly as I can, trying to catch my breath.

"We need to find shelter," he says.

I want to argue, to say that we should try again, but I know I can't. Not just yet. I need time to recover. And he's right, we can't stay out here in this. It's too dangerous and honestly, too damn miserable.

I can't get dry no matter how much fire I build in myself, and that isn't much at the moment. I need to save my magic for later.

I try to stand, but dizziness overtakes me, so Sebastian lifts me into his strong arms and carries me instead. I wrap my hands around his neck and let my head fall to his shoulder. He's wet, we both are, but he feels so solid and safe I smile as I close my eyes and he begins to walk towards the closest mountain.

It feels like we are trekking through a tornado, not that I specifically know what that's like, but I imagine it to be like this. Without Sebastian's earth magic and strength, I'm positive we'd be swept up in the air currents like Dorothy and Toto.

We walk for what feels like forever before we reach our destination. Sebastian scans the area and grunts. "I'm going to have to make us a cave to take shelter in," he says.

I just nod. It's all I can do at this point.

But I feel as he pulls at his power, channeling it at the base of the towering snow-peaked mountain.

Rocks grind and dirt shifts beneath us, and it sounds as if there's an earthquake. Feels that way too, but Sebastian holds on tight to me and I pry my eyes open to watch as a hole forms where once rock and dirt filled. He walks us into the new cavern and uses more magic to cover the opening with thick vines that block out the wind and rain. It's a small space with crystal stalactites hanging from the ceiling.

Sebastian props me against the wall. "Stay here, I'm going to get us some supplies."

I don't have time to ask what kind of supplies when he's gone, dashing away using his vampire speed.

He's back in record time with wood and animal fur. "Um, did you just go hunting?" I ask.

"No, the bear was already dead. I just borrowed his pelt."

Somehow the Earth Druid has also cleaned it so that it was not covered in the blood and guts of said bear. A gesture I was grateful for. He quickly gets to work building a small fire in the center, laying the fur to the side for me to use.

I summon the last of my strength to dry us both, against his objections, and then I lean against him as the fire before us blazes to life, warming the cave and casting lights off the crystals surrounding us.

"You saved this world," he says against my ear, his arms wrapped around me as I snuggle against him. "Again," he adds.

"It was a group effort," I say sleepily, the warmth of the fire, the steady drone of the rain and the feel of Sebastian's body all working together to lull me into unconsciousness.

"Led by you," he clarifies. "You're the bravest, most selfless person I've ever met."

I look up at him and caress his handsome face, losing myself in his forest green eyes. "Meeting you changed my life," I say. "That day on the subway, I had lost hope. I didn't know where I was headed or what my life would look like after Adam died. I had nothing left. Then I saw you, full of color and life, juxtaposed against a world of grey, and I couldn't stop thinking about you. Your eyes pulled me in to a new world, before I ever knew how literal that new world would be. You gave me a reason to live again. You saved me," I say. "So whatever you think of me, know that part of that is because of you."

He bends forward to press his forehead to mine. "You saved all of us," he says softly. "We would be dead right now if not for you."

Tears burn my eyes as I remember how close I had come to losing all of them. "Then we have saved each other. And now, we will save all of the Otherworld, and free it from the tyranny of the Mother of Dragons."

His lips find mine and despite my exhaustion, I can't help but respond in kind, pressing myself against him, intertwining my fingers into his hair as he claims my mouth with his. His arms pull me closer to him, and our bodies press together, feeding on each other's warmth and energy. I feel the stabling strength of his earth magic flow into me, giving my own powers a boost, giving me energy, healing me. And I melt into him as he moans against my mouth.

"Eve," he says breathlessly, pushing me away gently. "I want you, but I don't want to hurt you."

I push myself against him, again. "You could never hurt me."

And it's true, I realize. It has always been true. From the beginning, Sebastian has been my rock. The foundation that this entire new life was built upon. Without him, none of it would exist for me. Without him, I would still be sorting through the tattered shreds of my old life wondering how I ended up there, wondering where to go next. It was Sebastian's strength that has helped me heal from the death of my brother. His steadfastness that has gotten me through these recent trials and struggles. Even now, as the winds blow outside, as the world feels as if its ending, it's his arms around me that are holding me together, filling the holes in my magic, mending the tears in my heart.

"It has always been you," I say, and then there is no more space for words.

There are some emotions that are too powerful to be contained in words. They require the entire body to act as their language. To communicate the depths of my love for this man, I use everything I am. Body, mind, and soul.

Any walls between us crumble and new roots form, binding us, connecting us forever.

The power we share fills me with a new kind of strength that I grab onto with everything in me.

The fire crackles beside us, the crystals shining above us and I straddle the sexy Earth Druid, enjoying the feeling of him between my legs as my weariness evaporates as quickly as dew when the sun comes out.

His lips trail down my neck. "I have missed the feeling of the sun since being turned, but being with you is better than the warmest day, then the freshest morning breeze. You bring light into my life, joy into my heart. "You are my sun, Eve Oliver. You are my everything."

He whispers these words against my collar bone,

against my lips, against the hollow of my neck, and my skin absorbs his promises like a thirsty child on a hot summer day drinks his water. His declarations quench the thirst of my soul and fill me with love so deep and joy so pure I can't contain it. I feel it spilling out of me, shining through my skin like magic.

I look down at us and realize we are both glowing a golden light that radiates throughout the cave.

As he hardens beneath me, I realize we have too many clothes on, so I pull my arms away from him to quickly shimmy out of my shirt, until my breasts are free and tantalizingly close to his mouth.

He claims one of my nipples in his mouth and sucks, and my undressing is paused as pleasure strikes me like lightning, zapping through my body, spreading warmth everywhere.

I need to feel more of his flesh, so I tug at his shirt until he helps me get it off. I place my hands on his chiseled chest, enjoying the roped contours of his muscles. God he feels so good.

My breasts brush up against his bare skin and tighten in need. I grind against him but our pants are in the way of our pleasure, and there's no easy way of undoing this.

Unless...

I close my eyes and imagine just teleporting our pants and nothing else.

This is new for me.

But my power has returned. Being with him has strengthened me beyond what I could have imagined.

And in a blink, we are both naked, our clothes lying next to us now.

His eyes widen. "Neat trick." His voice is thick with desire, as he presses himself between my legs.

He resumes his attention to my breasts and drops his hand between my legs to heighten my need with his fingers.

At first, his touches are feather light, teasing my flesh. I arch closer to him as his tongue flicks at my nipple. When he presses his fingers deeper into me, I moan, desperate for more, unable to stop from moving my hips to feel him more deeply.

"I need you," I beg, ready for more than just fingers and tongue.

He groans, his mouth tracing a line of fire back up my chest to my neck.

He removes his fingers and uses both hands to grab my ass as I reposition myself to take him into me.

The moment I do, his teeth sink into my neck, and I cry out his name and thrust my hips, taking him as deeply as I can, my knees digging into the fur, our bodies pressed together, everything else disappearing but us.

It feels as if the entire mountain erupts as pleasure explodes within me and we both crash into each other, riding the high together as the storm thunders outside.

Spent and panting, we lay in each other's arms

beside the fire, and I run a finger over his chest as my head lays on his shoulder and his arms grip me firmly. My legs are wrapped around his and I relish the feeling of our skin-to-skin contact.

He kisses me and smiles. "That was definitely worth the wait."

I laugh and kiss him again. "It's the first of many," I say. "We will get through this, and we will have life-times to enjoy each other."

THE PLAN

Lying, thinking
 Last night
 How to find my soul a home
 Where water is not thirsty
 And bread loaf is not stone
 I came up with one thing
 And I don't believe I'm wrong
 That nobody,
 But nobody
 Can make it out here alone.
 ~Maya Angelou

WE BOTH FALL ASLEEP, and when we wake, the fire has died down, as has the storm. I sit up and stretch, grinning through a yawn. "That was…"

"Incredible," he says, kissing me and pulling me against him.

When he hardens against my stomach, I moan. "We should get back," I say, but it's not a convincing argument.

I'm ready for round two, and clearly, so is he.

With the first wave of passion spent, we now take our time. He explores my body slowly, studying the dips and valleys with his mouth, using his tongue rather than his fingers to tease me.

And when he enters me, it is deliberate, our gazes locked on each other, and a well of emotion consumes me, like the view from the top of a mountain after a long and arduous hike. I have waited so long for him, so long to feel him inside me, to complete this dance we started on the Subway in what feels like another life.

I wrap my legs around him and take him all the way in, enjoying the slow, delicious way he moves within me.

This time when we climax, it is like hang gliding off a mountain. His hands are gripped in mine, pinning them to the fur. My breasts are pressed to his chest, his lips are on mine. We are one.

We cuddle after for as long as we can justify it, then we reluctantly collect our clothing and dress.

"I'm guessing everyone will be worried sick about us," I say.

He shrugs, then winks at me. "Still worth it."

I chuckle. "You know I always wondered how people in thriller movies could take time from being stalked and nearly killed to have sex, but now I get it. In life or death situations, you realize the importance of that intimacy more than ever." I walk over to him and lay my hands on his chest. "If the world is going to end, I needed to be with you today, and as many times as I can before that happens."

"We are not going to let the world end," he says, frowning. "Because I don't think any of us will survive this life without you."

I blink away the tears when I realize what he's saying. "You have to," I whisper. "Alina needs you. You have to make it. For her. For me. Swear it."

He closes his eyes, his face a portrait of grief to come. "I swear it." He opens his eyes and caresses my face. "But know this. I will do whatever must be done to save you."

I know what he's saying, and I frown. "Let's first try it my way. Before we talk about turning over the child, let's try to find out what's going on with her powers and why. Let's find another way."

He nods and leads me out of the cave by the hand. But before we leave, I grab the fur. "For later," I say, winking.

He chuckles. "For later."

Outside, evidence of the storm is everywhere we look. Trees are toppled, pulled from their roots or split in half like twigs. Foliage is ripped out of the ground.

Boulders have been tossed about like pebbles. In short, it's a mess.

"We'd better get home, make sure everyone's okay," I say, reaching for Sebastian's hand.

"Are you sure you're strong enough to teleport?" he asks.

"It's easier than walking from... " I look around. "From wherever we are. Do you even know where we are?" I ask.

"No, not really. This must be part of the new world we haven't been to yet."

"Okay, well then we teleport. Besides, I feel as good as new." And it's true. I've made a remarkable recovery and feel stronger than ever.

It only takes me a moment to take us back to the castle, and we land by the front door, just as intended. Sebastian sways a bit and then steadies himself. "That's still very strange," he admits.

"I think it must be easier if you have Darkness," I say. "Otherwise you're fighting the magic."

He nods and the moment we step in the door we are greeted by three very worried men, two babies, and a pacing Dryad.

Derek pulls me into his arms. "We've been worried out of our minds. Where have you two been?"

I explain our confrontation with the Mother of Dragons, then the storm, then my powers conking out followed by our makeshift habitat for the night.

"Good thinking," Elijah says to Sebastian. "The cave was smart. That storm was the worst this world has ever seen. Buildings are damaged. People are panicking."

Lily steps forward. "Kaya says more people than ever are requesting transport to Earth. Especially those who can pass as human. Everyone knows something's up here, most just don't know how serious it is."

"What does Kaya say about the chances of getting everyone out if we need to," I ask.

Lily frowns. "It would take at least a month to evacuate this world, but that would create a massive influx in Earth that could trigger a whole new witch hunt."

"In other words, it would be a massacre the moment they arrived," I say.

Lily nods.

"So we have no choice," Derek says. "We need to turn the girl over."

"I don't think you understand," I say to Derek. "She's not going to leave this world intact. I'm sure of it. Once she has the murderer and her grandchild, she'll take her kids and head to her world, and snap her fingers to get rid of this one. I know it. I can see it in her."

They look at each other, and Liam shakes his head. "Eve is a Fate. If she sees this, we have to trust her."

Sebastian comes to my side. "I believe Eve as well," he says, surprising me. "I saw how unhinged the queen was. She will not leave us alone until we defeat her."

Elijah frowns. "You realize that's impossible, right?

I have searched every book I can get my hands on. There's nothing powerful enough to defeat her in this world."

"There has to be a way," I say, standing. "I'm going to visit a friend. I have an idea. I'll be back soon."

I close my eyes and imagine the place I want to go, then I open them and find myself standing before an ornate door carved of cherry wood. I use the door knocker and a moment later, a young woman with cat ears and a tale opens it. She's wearing a white fur jumpsuit and smiles when she sees me. "Eve!" she hugs me, and I laugh as I return the hug.

"You look happy," I say, so pleased she seems to be settling in well to her new life, after being a sex slave to The Collector.

"I am, thanks to you." She turns to escort me in. "Mistress Lilith will be delighted to see you."

"Hopefully that's still true after she finds out why I'm here," I say.

Lilith's mansion is a vision of class and sophistication, much like the ancient vampire herself.

She's sitting at a white grand piano in her all white living room, playing a complicated piece I don't recognize. She stops when she notices us, and stands, adjusting her crimson red dress as she walks over to greet us.

She looks like a drop of blood in her pristine parlor, and the contrast is striking. Lilith is one of those beings who always stands out from their environment, but in a way that is complimentary, as if the world is orientating itself around her.

"Eve, how lovely to see you," she says, kissing both my cheeks, then offering me a glass of wine.

"Actual wine, I hope?" I say, sniffing at it.

She laughs. "Of course, darling. I know you haven't yet developed a taste for the finer things. But give it time."

It's my turn to laugh. "I think I'm good, thanks though."

We sit across from each other and she leans back and studies me, her long sharp nails clicking against her wine glass which is definitely not filled with actual wine.

"It's been ages since you've come by for a visit. I hear you've been digging in the dirt with the peasants."

"Your elitism is almost offensive," I say smoothly, "were it not for the fact that I know you donated the money to feed and clothe everyone for nearly two months while we worked."

She wrinkles her nose. "How did you find out? It was meant to be anonymous."

"You just told me," I say, winking.

She rolls her eyes. "I cannot believe that trick worked on me. I must be losing my edge in my old age."

Lilith might be the oldest person alive, or undead, rather, but she looks in her prime, with flawless skin and luminous dark eyes that are keenly intelligent and full of secrets.

I fill her in on the details of my life the past few months, then I get to the crux of it. "I need your help."

"Of course you do," she says. "You have that look about it. Always getting into some kind of mischief. It's part of why I adore you. It's never boring when you're around."

"The dead dragon body count would disagree," I say.

"Tragic, truly, but still not boring."

To Lilith, boring is the worst offense. I guess when you've lived that long, everything else is just shades of perspective.

I decide to say this as bluntly as possible. "The world will end in less than two weeks, and I will die with it, unless we can defeat the Mother of the Dragons. Will you help me find a way to stop her?"

Lilith leans forward, putting her glass of blood down. "Oh my, this truly is the most excitement I've had in quite sometime. Amora is back is she? I had a fling with her once ages ago, but she is too racist for my taste."

"Is there anyone you haven't slept with?" I ask with a laugh.

She winks. "You, for one."

"Well, if we don't stop her soon, I won't be around as an option for much longer."

"Then I guess we're going to have to play chess with the most powerful being in all the worlds I know of," she says with a conniving smile. "And in this game, there is no king."

I take a sip of my wine before asking, "Where do we start? How do we get to her?" I tell her about the unicorn horn dagger I have, and her eyes widen.

"How did you come across one of those? I thought they'd all been destroyed during the war."

"War?" I ask. "I thought it was more like a slaughter?"

Lilith shrugs sipping her blood. "The unicorns killed off many dragons in other worlds before coming here. They had their horns set on the Council, but before that could happen, the Council got wise and had them killed off first. So, who's the villain in that story? It's impossible to say. War begets war begets war. It's the same with all races and species on all worlds."

That's news to me, and something Callia didn't share. I wonder why.

"Elijah says there's nothing in the world he can find that will kill a dragon like her," I say.

A mischievous sparkle lights up Lilith's eyes. "Then we'll need to look outside of this world."

"Earth," I ask, doubtfully.

She shakes her head. "Only the Dragon's own world will have the answers, I fear. But fortunately, I still have a secret way in, thanks to our long ago tryst. I'll go, do some digging, see what I can find, and come back. In the meantime, go prepare yourself for the battle ahead. This is going to be one hell of a ride, and we can't have you damaging that gorgeous face of yours."

I'm still chuckling at her childlike enthusiasm for war as I blink and send myself back to the castle.

No one is downstairs, so I venture out back to check on Ana. She's curled in a corner playing with her doll.

"Hey there, honey. How are you?" I ask.

She shrugs, not speaking.

Gods I feel like such an ass.

"Are you hungry? I can get you some food."

She shakes her head.

"Do you want me to read you a story?" I ask, though I don't have time for that, but I'll make it work for this poor kid.

She shakes her head again.

I sigh. "Okay, I'll come check on you soon."

I glance at the bushes on my way back in and see that Racul's body has been removed. The memory of him throwing himself in front of me to take the blow sends shivers up my spine, and I still don't know how to factor that Dath'Racul against the giant ass from court. People—and dragons—aren't always what you think.

I head upstairs, hoping there's not more bad news awaiting me. I fear the worst as I approach Matilda's room, but when I push open the door, my heart warms to see all four brothers sitting around her bed as they talk. She has tears running down her weathered cheeks, and Liam holds her hand. The babies are in a crib in the corner napping.

I don't want to interrupt, so I pull the door closed behind me and head to my room to take a bath and have a minute alone before reality sets in too hard and we must make our next plan.

Moon is excited to see me, and curls around my ankles purring as I prepare my bath. I pick him up and hold him against my chest, enjoying the velvety softness of his fur.

He takes his customary spot at the edge of my tub as I heat the water with my magic and step in.

I try to pause my mind for just a few minutes. To forget about the end of the world and the dead dragons, and the monster killer who's just a child. I push it all away and meditate on just the present moment. The bubbles tickling my skin. The heat of the water soaking away my weariness. The scent of lavender oil. The sound of Moon purring.

"You look like a goddess," a familiar voice says, startling me out of my meditative state.

I sit up with a jerk, splashing water over the sides of the tub as Cole Night saunters over and takes a seat next to me, my bathrobe in his hands.

"What are you doing here?" I ask, my heart palpitating at his presence. And even though I really don't want to want him. I totally want him. Damn this man and the effects he has on me.

"I heard you have a problem with a queen. I'm here to help."

I sigh. "It truly is impossible to keep secrets around here."

I stand and grab my robe from his hands, slipping into it as I climb out of the tub.

Then I realize there's other news he may or may not know. "Matilda... " I say, unsure how to proceed.

"I know she was attacked," he says softly.

"Yes, but she's okay now I think. But that's not all," I say, struggling to find the right words.

Understanding dawns on his face and he nods. "So, she finally told you?" he asks.

I narrow my eyes. "Told me what?"

"That she's a Fate."

"No! She didn't tell me, but yes, I did find out. I had a memory of it. But how the hell did you know?" I ask, confused.

We walk back into my bedroom, and I take a seat in front of the fire as Moon makes a spot on my lap. Cole takes the chair next to me. "I didn't know for sure, but I've suspected for some time. She's always had visions and known things she shouldn't. She's been around forever but no one has ever really known what she is, or where her power comes from. It just made sense."

"Why didn't you tell your brothers? Or me?"

"For one, it wasn't my secret to tell. Matilda had her reasons for keeping her identity to herself and I wasn't going to betray that. And two, I didn't know for sure.

Also, it's not like my brothers and I have been close," he says.

"Why aren't you angry with her if you've stayed angry with your brothers for so long?"

"Because I don't know what her direct role was in what happened to me. I know what theirs was."

"Oh Cole," I say, my heart breaking for him all over again. "They aren't the same men they were back then. They weren't strong enough to fight the powers that controlled your lives."

"And they are now?" he asks bitterly.

"We're all stronger," I say. "Together." I look pointedly at him. "I'm working on a plan to stop the Mother of Dragons, but I'll need everyone's help. Including yours. We can't do this without you. Can I count on you to help?"

Cole looks at me, his dark eyes hypnotizing and full of so much pain. "I'll do what I can. But this isn't a battle that will be easily won. What's your plan?" he asks.

"Like I said, I'm still working on it." Sheesh, doesn't anyone listen? "But I'm open to suggestions."

THE GOODBYES

"Goodbyes are only for those who love with their eyes. Because for those who love with heart and soul there is no such thing as separation."
    Rumi

COLE JOINS HIS BROTHERS, spending time with Matilda, and when they are done, we all meet in the library and spend hours brainstorming ways to defeat the queen, but the fact is we just don't know enough. We only know one way to kill her—the unicorn dagger —but no one has a solid plan for how to get it into her heart, which seems to be the sure fire way to get the job done. Ra'Terr was simply injured with a horn, and his death is coming slowly, too slowly to stop the queen.

It's a tedious back and forth that ends with Cole jumping up in frustration. "We should all just leave.

Get out of here. Get as many people off this world as possible, sure, but then we leave. We can't win this."

"He doesn't know?" Liam asks.

I shake my head. I really don't want to have this conversation. Again. But it seems I must.

And so I tell Cole what everyone else now knows. That I won't survive the destruction of this world.

That silences him, and without saying another word, he storms out of the library.

I lean back in the couch and close my eyes, pinching the bridge of my nose to alleviate a headache. The fire crackles and candles are lit around the room creating an ambiance I don't feel. I'm tired of arguing. Of planning. Of worrying.

Standing, I pick up Alina from the crib and hold her against my chest. Her baby fists reach for anything they can grab, settling for a bit of my shirt that she tries to shove into her mouth.

"I'm going for a walk," I say.

Sebastian stands. "I'll join you, if that's all right?"

I nod. "Only if you promise not to mention anything related to end of the world shit. I need a mental break."

"Agreed."

Elijah stands and stretches. "I think you're right. We're talking in circles. I'll keep researching and see if I can find anything in my books. But there might not be an easy solution to this."

"There might not be any solution to this," Liam says, his brow creased in worry.

"Then we do what we can," I say. "And we keep on living until then. What else is there?"

Derek frowns but doesn't say what I know he's thinking. That we could at least try and turn over Ana. It might work.

But I know it won't. I feel it so deeply within me that it's more than just a hunch, or even a flash. It's a Fate premonition, or whatever that is.

The evening is chilly, and I wear a cloak and wrap Alina in a blanket before putting her in the stroller.

Moon joins us as we head to the gardens and stroll over the cobbled paths that wind around the property.

Sebastian pushes the baby and I loop my arm into his as we walk slowly, enjoying the stillness of the night. While there is no sun and moon in this world, and the shift from day to night is much more subtle, I've lived here long enough to understand the different shades of color and light in the Dragon's Breath.

We stop beneath a weeping willow near a pond and I take Ana out and spread a blanket for her so she can stretch, then Sebastian and I lean against the tree and I tuck myself into his arms and try to clear my mind of everything but this moment.

It occurs to me we are never guaranteed a future, whether it's measured in minutes, years or lifetimes. Anything could happen, and so all we can do is stay as present as we can in the moments we are assured.

So I take it all in. The baby playing at our feet. The black cat curled up next to me. The beautiful man at my side. The fish swimming in the pond. The birds flying overhead.

All of it is a miracle.

"What are you thinking about?" Sebastian asks after a time.

I tilt my head up to him to look into his gorgeous green eyes. "You. Us. The wonder of it all. I've been given more than I ever thought possible. No matter how long it lasts, I can't complain."

A flood of emotions fills us both and he kisses me, drawing out my love for him, his love for me, in that one intimate exchange.

Then Alina begins to cry and we pull away from each other and laugh.

Sebastian checks her diaper and crinkles his nose. "I'll take her back to the house and give her a bath before putting her to bed."

I nod. "I'll be back in a bit."

I watch them walk away, then I head towards the ocean, Moon still at my heels. He seems to know something's up and hasn't wanted to leave my side lately.

Despite not wanting to dwell on what could be, I know I need to make plans if the worst-case scenario happens. So, I make a list in my mind of what that will look like. People I need to talk to. Letters I need to write. People I want to draw before my time might be up.

Was this how Adam felt as he was contemplating the end of his life? Did he look at his life lived and weigh what he would need to do to close out the final chapter?

The ocean air invigorates me, and I slip my shoes off and stand at the shore, letting the water lap over my toes as Moon dashes back and forth, dodging the tide, then chasing it when it flees.

"Are you really so connected to this world that your life will end if it does?" Cole asks from behind me.

I should be used to him just turning up randomly, but the man still startles me.

I turn around, frowning. "I wouldn't lie about this."

He shrugs. "It would be a good way to motivate my brothers to stay and help."

I huff at that. "They don't need my potential demise to want to save thousands of others," I say. "They are good men with good hearts."

"Unlike me," he says softly.

I consider him a moment before replying. "Our goodness lies in our choices, which means we are, each moment, given opportunities to reinvent ourselves. You can be whoever you choose to be."

"I wish I believed that," he says, staring into the ocean.

"Have you come to say goodbye again?" I ask, my heart hurting.

"I don't know why I'm here, except that whenever

I'm away from you too long, a heaviness grows in me that I cannot carry."

"Then stay," I say simply, but I know he will not. It is not yet who he is choosing to be.

"Can I kiss you?" he asks, and I'm surprised, not by the fact that he wants this, but that he asked permission.

I answer by turning to him and tilting my head up.

His arms encircle my waist, landing low on my hips as he steps closer to me, so that our bodies are pressed together.

My darkness reaches for his, my light as well, the two mingling with his dual magic, and the completion I feel at his closeness is a bittersweet balm that soothes even as it burns. I feel my heart breaking again, just a little, as he teases at my lips, tasting me. I slide my arms over his shoulders, through his thick black hair, deeming the kiss he began, tasting him in all his darkness and light.

And I feel the moment he begins to dematerialize, disintegrating like mist in my arms. When I open my eyes, he is gone, and I wonder if I will ever see Cole Night again.

OVER THE NEXT FEW DAYS, I bury myself in my art. I feel a compulsion to draw, to create portraits of the people I love most in the world. I try not to view it as saying goodbye, but there's no denying there is an element of that in all that I do.

Still, I'd like to think that I would have come to this place eventually, that space within myself where I see how important it is to show people how you feel about them before it's too late.

I still haven't heard from Lilith, and none of the brothers have found anything new, so our plan basically relies on luck.

With that in mind, I teleport myself to Kaya's grove where I know Lily will be.

I find the two of them leaning against Kaya's massive tree, arms intertwined, love glowing in them both.

When Lily sees me, she frowns and stands. "Eve! Is everything okay? Did something happen?"

"No, everyone is fine. I just... " I pause. This is harder to do than I'd imagined. "Can we talk? All three of us," I ask, glancing at Kaya.

They invite me to join them and I take a seat on the soft mossy earth and pull out the drawing I have for them. "I made this for the two of you," I say, handing it to them.

It's one of my most unique drawings, done on a large dried leaf using only pigments made from natural sources. I've secured it to a piece of wood that was donated by one of the trees I worked with in the new world. It's a portrait of both of them, their more human forms in front, with their trees behind them.

Lily's eyes fill with tears. "This is amazing. Thank you!" She leans over to hug me and I squeeze her tight, then pull away.

"There's something else," I say. "I need you to promise me something."

She nods, and Kaya holds her hand.

"If this showdown with the queen goes south, as it very well could, I need you to get our family and our friends out of this world as quickly as possible. The Nights, the kids, the Ifrits, the Gargoyles, Lilith and her household, everyone. Can you do that?"

"You mean if the world ends and you die?" she asks softly.

"Yes. That's what I mean."

Tears fill her eyes and she looks to Kaya, who nods. "We will," Kaya says as Lily swipes at a tear. "You have our word."

Relief floods me. Knowing my loved ones will be safe makes this a little easier, though I wish there was a way I could save everyone in this world, not just the ones I know personally. It's not fair or right, but I'm doing my best. This is all just a shit situation however you look at it.

I take Lily's hand. "I'm so glad to know you," I say. "You are full of life and love and laughter, and you have become one of the best friends I have ever had. Thank you."

We spend the afternoon visiting, walking through the groves and talking about our lives, then I head to the Mausoleum and repeat this all with my friends there.

Okura and Akuro greet me first, landing before me when I materialize at the entrance. The baby is with them and I show them the portrait I created for the three of them. This one is etched into stone, which seemed fitting.

I don't know if Gargoyles decorate or enjoy this kind of thing, but I wanted to do something for them.

They are speechless. "I've never seen a likeness made of our family like this," Okura admits, her deep voice thick with emotion. "Our kind doesn't really get gifts. Ever."

"I hope I haven't offended you with this," I say, wondering if I should have checked the protocol first.

"Not at all," Akuro says. "We are pleased."

I take the baby when Okura offers her to me and cuddle her. Well, as much as you can cuddle animated stone.

I also hand them a Memory Catcher. "Please do not watch this unless something happens to me."

Okura frowns. "Is something meant to happen to you?"

I give a sad smile. "None of us are guaranteed a tomorrow. But if the worst happens, watch it and you'll know what to do."

I swear I see a tear slide down Okura's stony cheek as I enter the Mausoleum.

Ifi and Elal aren't in the morgue, so I head to their apartment, and there I find them cooking dinner.

Their door is left open, likely to air out the smoke building in their home.

"What are you two doing?" I ask, choking as I use a bit of air magic to help clear out the kitchen.

"Oh thank the gods you are here," Elal says, sounding more like Ifi than himself. "My husband has decided to take up cooking. That's normally my job but he insisted he wants to be more helpful in the kitchen." Elal waves a hand as if to say, 'look how helpful he's being.'

I chuckle. "At least he's trying."

Ifi huffs as he stirs a large pot. "I am creating a masterpiece. Both of you take a seat at the table and stop your whining. A little smoke never hurt anyone."

I could cite studies that would disagree with that, but instead I follow Elal to the table and we both sit, eyeing the Ifrit nervously as he serves up whatever is in the pot into large bowls that he places before us with a flourish.

"Now, dine on the most magnificent food you will ever experience in your lives," he says.

Whatever is in the bowl... and I really do mean *whatever*... is green and slimy, and my stomach flops over at the thought of introducing it to this substance of questionable edibility.

"Um, Ifi," I say, not quite sure how to phrase this. "You know that though I'm a Fate, I'm still in a mostly human body, right? So, I have to be careful what I put inside it, lest I end up on your table prematurely."

He cocks his hip and rolls his eyes. "I know, I know. Rude. I assure you, this is safe for human consumption."

Elal moves the gelatinous sludge around with a spoon, not looking the least bit convinced by his husband's encouragement.

He looks up at me. "Ladies first?"

I fall back on my standard line in this world. "Age before beauty."

"How about we do this together?" Elal proposes as a compromise. "On three?"

"Fine."

"One. Two. Three."

I take the smallest taste I can, while still managing to get some on the spoon. I'm definitely expecting to gag. Possibly die.

The flavor takes a moment to hit, and when it does, I see Elal's eyes widen just as mine do.

I take another bite just to make sure I'm not hallucinating, and yep, I was right. "Ifi, this truly is amazing."

Elal nods his head. "The key is not looking at it while eating it, I think," he says, patting his husband on the hand.

Ifi walks back to the kitchen, beaming. "I told you. Best chef ever."

"Can we work on the presentation?" I ask, avoiding direct eye contact with the green goo while I eat.

"I'll see what I can do."

We visit for a bit before I pull out the sketch I made for them. This one was a bit tricky to create, and I actually used my magic for the first time while drawing. I hand them a piece of wood with their portrait burned into it. In it, they are looking at each other with such love and devotion, you can feel it in your heart.

Ifi starts crying the moment he sees it, and Elal pulls his husband into his arms.

"This is just the most touching gift we've ever gotten," Ifi says. "And I look hot!" Then he looks to Elal. "So do you, of course."

Elal smiles. "Of course."

Our goodbyes are bittersweet, and when I hand them their Memory Catcher, they know what it contains, but Elal pockets it anyways. "This isn't the end," he whispers as he hugs me. "You may be a Fate, but you're also a Phoenix at heart. You will always rise from the ashes to be reborn."

His words stay with me long after I leave.

OVER THE NEXT few days I wait to hear from Lilith. I have a portrait for her as well, drawn with blood, which was... an interesting medium. In the picture, she's at the tree of knowledge licking blood off an apple while a snake slithers around her ankles. I am eager to show her the gift, but Lilith is still not back from her trip.

And then finally, the day has come. We have run out of time, and our plan is iffy at best.

"One hour," Liam says, staring into the dancing flames of the fire.

"Lily and Kaya will be here soon to take the kids away," I say. We decided it would be best for them to be out of the world ahead of time, just in case. I wish I could convince the Night brothers to go as well, but without them to help me, we don't stand a chance, and we need to try at least. Too many lives are at stake.

I walk over to Alina and pull her from the crib, cuddling her against me. I try not to cry as I imagine what will happen if we don't succeed.

The Night brothers surround us, forming a group hug with me and the baby in the center. Their power flows through me and I soak it up, hoping it will be enough.

Lily enters the room, Kaya at her side. "We're ready," she says.

I hand Alina to Kaya and Lily goes to pick up Zara who instantly starts screaming. She shifts from baby to dragon form, and her screams become the shouts of a dragon in distress. They echo throughout the castle and reverberate in our bones. Water begins spewing from her mouth, and Alina joins in, screaming, crying, thrashing and throwing fire balls indiscriminately.

"What the hell is going on?" Liam shouts over the noise.

"I have no idea," I say, scrambling to catch Alina's fire and neutralize it before she burns the damn castle down. "They were fine a second ago."

"Maybe they know we're trying to take them away," Lily says, nearly dropping Zara when the baby dragon spreads her wings and tries to fly.

The pitch of the dragon scream changes and nearly splits my eardrums, and then my flash buzzes and I clutch my head. "Oh, shit."

Outside, thunder rattles the rooftop as a new storm brews from a previously clear sky, and the sound of dragon wings fills the air.

A loud roar shakes the foundation of the castle and a dreadful cracking sound is the only warning we have before the entire top half of the castle is torn off to show a giant golden dragon looking down at us, lightning pouring from her. "Give me my grandchild!"

THE STORM

"Love makes the ocean boil like a pot. Love grinds mountains down to sand. Love splits the heaven into a hundred pieces. Love shakes the earth with a mighty shaking...If not for pure love, why would I give existence to the spheres? I raised the Celestial wheel on the high so that you might understand love's elevation."
~Rumi

WITH THE LOWER LEVEL OF the castle now exposed to the elements, rain pelts us, soaking everything. Lily backs away, still holding a screaming baby dragon.

Everything is chaos.

Before the Night brothers and I can scramble to protect the kids, the queen of dragons shoots a bolt of golden light at Lily, hitting her in the arm and knocking her down. Zara attempts to fly unsteadily, then drops to the ground crying. Kaya looks frantically between Alina in her arms, and her unconscious lover on the floor. I try to distract the queen to give the dryad a chance to help them both.

"Amora!" I say, filling myself with power, my voice projecting into the heavens. "Stop! We have not harmed your grandchild." I think quickly, trying to mitigate the damage. "We were about to bring her to you at the meeting time. Why are you attacking us?"

"You lie," roars the queen, flames flicking from her lips. Her golden eyes look past me, to Matilda on what remains of the balcony, who is dressed in her Fate robes for the first time since I've known her. The Queen sneers, "Another Fate. I remember you, though you now deign to show your face. Your kind has brought me nothing but pain. This world ends now!" She begins chanting, her voice echoing on the wind, and her body begins to glow like the sun.

Callia appears by my side. "You must kill her. Now. It's the only way," she says.

"No." I'm not a murderer. We can still execute my plan.

"Elijah." I call out. "Sebastian. Liam. Derek. It's time."

The Night brothers snap into action, rushing to my side as we discussed. We all clasp hands and form a circle. The earth druid to my right. The water druid to my left. Fire and air across from me.

I channel my powers, seeking to create a barrier like the one I did to hold Ana. I only had a few of the brothers lending me their strength that time. With all four it should be enough to hold even the Mother of Dragons. It must be enough. The elements swirl together, creating an intricate web of white light that covers the giant dragon. Magic seals, runes that I once knew in a past life, begin to appear around her. The barrier is forming. Her glow diminishing. She is trapped.

Matilda manages to make her way downstairs and joins our circle as Kaya manages to take Lily, Alina and Zara outside the castle. The barrier strengthens, becoming almost blinding with its light, fueled by the power of two Fates and four druids.

But as the queen fights against her captivity, I can feel my magic stretching, pulling, and tearing apart. For a moment, I connect with the Queen, with her power, and I feel an energy so hot, so overwhelming, it burns like an inferno. A heat so blistering even a fire druid could not resist its flames. There is so much power here. More than I have ever felt. The blaze grows. The queen screams.

And the barrier shatters.

A shockwave erupts from the golden dragon, knocking all five of us to the ground, breaking our circle as wooden furniture splinters apart and stone cracks to pieces.

"I killed a Fate once," roars the queen. "You think I

can't kill more?" She resumes her chanting, and the ground beneath us begins to crack as the world is undone piece by piece.

The northern wall splits in half, crumbling under the weight of its own stone, and then it falls, leaving us in only a partial shell of a castle, our library now extending into the side garden.

I think of all the lives that will be lost and wonder if I could have done more. If I should have tried to save as many as possible before it came to this. But I don't have time to second guess myself.

I channel all my power, my body glowing white, and I float into the sky and summon lightning at my fingertips, flinging it at her, but the bolts bounce off her golden scales like pebbles.

I try fire next, and it slips off her like oil. Nothing is working.

Below me, Sebastian tries to hold the earth together. Elijah and Derek work as one to keep the storm from tearing us all apart. And Liam launches his own useless attack.

It's over.

Unless...

I tap into my Darkness, using the tracking spell Cole helped me to perform, and search for the unicorn dagger. It should be somewhere below. Amongst the rubble.

But it's not.

It's above me.

Close to the queen.

I don't understand.

Until I see the dark mist.

See his body appearing midair, black cloak flapping in the wind, unicorn dagger in hand.

Cole.

He materializes at her chest and plunge's the dagger toward her heart. It breaks through a scale, and the queen roars in agony, golden blood spilling from her wound, her wings flapping erratically. Cole places both hands on the hilt, driving the dagger deeper. Deep enough to pierce her heart.

But then she swipes at him with one of her massive talons, hitting him in the side. And like an insignificant mosquito, he is flung through the air, dagger slipping from his palm as it falls into the shadows. I create a pocket of wind to catch him, slowing his descent to the ground. His face is bloody and purple, but he manages a grin through scarlet lips.

The queen of dragon roars, holding a claw in front of her chest to protect her gaping wound. "I should have destroyed this cesspool without warning. It is over. You cannot defeat me. Give up!" Her voice carries through the sky and the destruction continues.

But then she glances behind us and her eyes widen. Her words stop. Her glow fades. For the first time, I see the dragon queen afraid. "No. It can't be. I killed you a millennium ago. You cannot be here. You're supposed to be dead."

I follow her gaze behind me, to the garden.

To the creature that is now free. A black and golden monstrosity, with wings that look crooked and torn, and a venomous drill-like horn. Ana. In her true form. She grows in size, flying towards the Queen—her mother.

How did she get out? But then I realize... the Queen freed her child herself when she tore apart the earth. It must have broken the magical seal we created.

The two clash in the sky, the dragon queen moving desperately to avoid her daughters horn, striking out with her claws, cutting into the hybrid-creature's shoulder. Ana cries out into the storm, a hideous sound of pain and anguish and fury.

And in that moment, with the Queen of Dragons and her abandoned child fixed completely on each other, I see my opportunity. I use my Darkness to track the dagger once more, and with my Air, I retrieve the blade, hovering in midair before me, and aim it at the Queen's heart.

That's it.

I have the shot.

All I need is a push.

But something shifts within me.

A struggle at my very core.

I've taken a life before. But my past self was in control then. The ancient Maiden Fate. But now... Now I am in control. The dragon's blood will be on my hands.

I can't take another life.

But I can't let her take my world.

"*In lumen et lumen*," I whisper.

And with flick of my wrist, the dagger flies true.

And penetrates the Queen's heart.

SHE SCREAMS and drops from the sky, but as she does, she shoots one last golden arch of lightning at Ana, hitting her in the heart.

They both land hard on the wet crumbling earth, creating a wave of earthquakes that is felt across the world.

I lower myself from the sky and race to them, praying it's over, that we are safe.

As I approach the Queen, she shifts into her human form, clutching the dagger in her heart. Golden blood seeps out of her wound and mouth, but still she smiles. "At least I will die knowing I am taking this wretched world with me. It is over. It is done. I have completed the spell to end the Otherworld."

I reel back, terrified, sickened, my soul feeling as if it's being sucked from my body. "What did you do?" I scream at the dying dragon. "What have you done?" I can't control my tears, or my rage, as her life fades away and my world continues to crumble.

Near her, Ana lies still. Too still. Her body now that of a little girl, but not as before. A small unicorn horn protrudes from her forehead and delicate dragon wings span out behind her.

I crawl over to the motionless form, my body hurting as if it too is being torn apart.

I am dying.

As the world dies, I too am becoming undone.

I take Ana's hand, and her eyes flicker open. "I remember now," she says, words barely a whisper. "But I didn't mean to. You have to believe me. I didn't mean to. My friend... she made me... " Her eyes flicker closed again, and she goes still. Her hand goes limp in mine.

I can't see through my tears. Through my pain. Through my rage.

And then the Night brothers, all five of them, surround me. They hold me, support me, and give me strength.

And a thought begins to form.

"What if... "

I look at them all. Each representing the elements that live within me.

I glance at Amora, whose body remains.

And I wonder.

"We can save the world," I shout over the storm. "But we have to work together."

I look to Cole, the prodigal brother, the lost soul. "We need you," I say.

Tears fill his dark eyes and he nods.

I glance at the rings on my fingers and trace the symbols of darkness and earth in the air. The Night

Brothers and I form a circle once more, all of us holding hands, but this time Cole is with us. Six elements. Like the six dragons who first formed this world. I recall the spell Ava'Kara taught me. The one I used to expand the Otherworld. But this time, I'll use Amora, the Mother of the Dragons, as the focal point.

"It won't work," Ra'Terr says, his body wrapped in his dark wings as he lands from the sky with Brock by his side. They glance quickly at their mother's corpse, and for a moment I see a hint of sadness in their eyes, but it is quickly gone, replaced by a hard resolve. "The sacrifice has to be from a living dragon." He clutches the poisonous wound at his side, leaning on his sister for support. "Use me," he says simply. "I can be the sacrifice."

Brock turns her head, auburn hair wild in the storm, emotion clouding her eyes. "No. You..."

"It's the only way," he says. "I'd rather die like this, then live a moment longer knowing I have failed my people. Use me. I will be the sacrifice. Let me amend for any harm I may have caused those I swore to protect."

I nod, tears streaming down my face and flying away in the wind, and I resume the spell, this time focused on Ra'Terr. Brock stands away, and they maintain eye contact with each other as I channel all the power the six of us have, into the body of Ra'Terr and into the body of this world.

The storm rages even stronger.

Wind nearly blinds me.

Debris flies through the air.

Still I scream out the words Ava'Kara taught me, infused with every ounce of magic I have left in my body.

"Terry autumn usque ad terram!"

Everything around the Darkness Dragon turns dark, like a black hole spreading from his body, consuming him. Within, a small spark of light begins to glow, growing brighter until it explodes like a dying sun, creating a shining dust that falls to the ground and dissipates into nothing.

Instantly, the storm dies down, the earth stops shaking, and the world becomes eerily silent.

THE FRIEND

Tell all the Truth but tell it slant –
  Success in Circuit lies
  Too bright for our infirm Delight
  The Truth's superb surprise
  ~Emily Dickinson

TWO WEEKS Later

THE DAYS PASS LIKE A DREAM. I am weak for many of them, drained from my spell, and nearly help-less when the people begin to rebuild what was broken. Two weeks pass before my strength returns, and it is time to go.

The Night brothers and I arrive in the grove early, but already it's crowded with Otherworlders of all kinds. Lily and Kaya are already there waiting for us, and hugs are exchanged as we take our places near the front. Matilda insisted on staying behind to care for the children, but I honestly think this was too much for her. She has kept her identity a secret for so long, I think it's hard for her to be known and to face her past. Healing will take time for everyone, but there is enough love to guide us through.

There's a sense of solemn festivity that often accompanies funerals, which are inherently strange, I've always thought. They are a blend of celebration, mourning, and socializing that lends itself to a singularly unique experience equivalent to an emotional milkshake. Throw every feeling you've ever had together and blend.

Brock'Mir stands on a platform built for this event. There are no bodies left of her siblings, so she asked me to paint portraits of each of them for the service. Those are placed around her as she addresses the crowd.

"Today we come to honor the sacrifices of my brothers and sisters, and to say goodbye to the Age of the Dragons."

A murmur spreads through the crowd as everyone wonders what that means.

"Ava'Kara was the first amongst us to die. She gave her life willingly to expand this world so that there would be room for everyone who needs sanctuary and safety. For all those who share our bloodline and our magic. We honor her."

There is a moment of silence as I use my magic to bring water up from the land, creating a natural fresh water source. It will flow always, giving refreshment to weary travelers in Kara's name.

"Lyx'Ara spent much of her later life living amongst you, helping you, leading many of you into what is called the New World. She believed in a system that recognized everyone as valid, as belonging, as deserving, and we honor her."

There is a moment of silence and I create a ball of pure white light that brightens the forest around us and will remain there always as a symbol of the light Lyx brought to the world.

"My brother, Ventus'Arak took his own life. In his final message to us, he expressed his deep grief over the unraveling of our world and our family. My heart breaks for his life, and I honor him."

This silence is the most painful for my heart. Suicide cuts twice as deep. But I pull my air magic out and allow a gentle breeze to caress the crowd. Anyone who ventures into this forest will feel the touch of the wind in the Air Dragon's memory.

"As many of you know, my brother Dath'Racul was also murdered, defending the life of one of the Fates. And we honor him."

I create a great bonfire with my magic, the fire burning brightly and providing heat to all around it. It is a fire that will never spread, but will always bring warmth and comfort to those who come here. Racul will be remembered.

"And finally, Ra'Terr gave his last moments of life to aid in saving this world from destruction. To save your lives. And we honor him."

In discussing with Brock how to honor her siblings, this was the hardest and required the most thought. I pull a strand of Darkness from my soul and cast a shadow in the shape of a dragon over the land near us. Anyone who walks through the darkness will feel the power of their own shadow self rise up in them, and will be encouraged to embrace that part of them to become whole.

"We come to the end of our ceremony," Brock says, "but there is one last thing that must be done. I am leaving the Otherworld."

There are gasps and protestations. People crying out asking who will lead them?

She waits until they die down before calling me over to her.

A lump forms in my throat as I walk onto the stage and take my place by her side, tugging at my purple cloak from my past life which Matilda altered to fit my current life.

"Eve Oliver is the Maiden Fate reborn."

This brings a few gasps, but I'm pretty sure that rumor has already spread everywhere.

"She contains within herself all the elements of each of the dragons."

That gets people talking.

"And she has saved our world, twice. First when she expanded it. Second when she stopped my mother from destroying it. Her life is bound to this world and to you. As my last act as High Dragon of the Council of Dragons, I name Eve Oliver my successor on this world and Guardian of the Otherworld."

She pulls from her robe a staff made of a deep black wood with a crystal tip. "Do you accept this responsibility and all it entails?" she asks me.

"I do," I say.

"Then it is done. Eve, Guardian of the Otherworld, High Priestess of the Council of Dragons, Maiden Fate Reborn. My people, you have a new leader, and I know you will be in the best of hands. The Age of Dragons is over, but a new age has arisen, and it is one for all the people of the Otherworld."

A great cheer fills the forest and I can't help the tears that flow down my cheeks. I look to the brothers, all five together, a family as we were always meant to be, and I feel their love and magic pouring into me.

LATER THAT NIGHT, after much celebrating, drinking and eating, we return to the castle with Brock, who looks as tired as I feel. "Are you sure you want to do this tonight?" I ask, for her sake but also mine. This goodbye will be hard.

She nods. "My people are waiting for me. My kingdom, in my true world, does not have a leader. Given my mother's frame of mind, perhaps they have not had one for a very long time. Now that I know my people here are safe, I need to take my place as Queen there."

We walk into the library where Zara and Alina are playing in the crib together. Matilda is asleep in a corner chair so we do not wake her. Liam picks up Zara and holds her close, kissing her forehead, then passes her to the other brothers.

And then she's given to me, and I hold her tightly and whisper words only meant for her before I hand her to her aunt.

"I wish she could stay with us forever," I say, "but I know she needs her own kind."

More tears flow, and the Earth Dragon looks on sympathetically. "I will bring her back for visits," she says, as Alina begins to cry when she realizes her best friend will not be returning.

Liam picks up his daughter and rocks her to soothe her feelings.

"And what of the girl," Brock says. "Ana?"

"She has shown no signs of the monster since that night," I say.

Liam nods. "All of my examinations have indicated that in her death, the monster part of her died and the child yet lived."

"A child who is part unicorn, part dragon," Brock says.

"Yes. And maybe one day she will exhibit shifting abilities," Elijah says, "but we have seen no evidence of this."

"So you will keep her and raise her?" Brock asks.

I look to the brothers and nod. "Yes. She is family now."

Brock smiles. "Very well. If she ever does show signs of shifting into a dragon, don't hesitate to reach out. She may need guidance from us to know herself."

"We won't," I assure her.

Tension coils in me as our time nears to an end.

And out of the corner of my eye, I see a small form sneaking through the shadows behind the Earth Dragon, wielding the unicorn horn dagger.

I hold out a hand and cast a shield, just as Ana strikes against the dragon, and trap her in a barrier before she can do any harm.

There's chaos for a moment as Sebastian pushes Brock out of the way and everyone stares wide eyed, shocked at the little girl holding the weapon mid-air, ready to kill the last remaining adult dragon on this world.

I remain calm.

And approach the child. "Ana? Can you hear me?"

But she doesn't respond. Her eyes are black pools floating in silver and I know she's not acting on her own accord.

She never was.

"Callia, show yourself!" I shout, and then I repeat

the words Lilith taught me. The mother of all vampires did not discover how to defeat Amora in her time away, but she did bring back some very useful information. And it helped me put all the pieces together.

Callia appears, locked in a barrier much like the one holding Ana, looking angry and confused. "How did you summon me against my will?" she demands. She thrashes, but no amount of force allows her to escape.

"You can't leave or hide any longer. You have been behind the murders the whole time, haven't you?"

Her eyes shift, and she realizes that everyone can now see her. Her mouth is agape as her new reality settles in on her. "I... how did you know?"

"I never believed Ana was acting out these attacks on her own. She was having night terrors and talked of an imaginary friend. I suspected she was being controlled, but didn't put the pieces together until Lilith returned from the dragon world with some very interesting information about the war between the unicorns and the dragons, and a specific ability the unicorns had to control other sentient beings, making them particularly dangerous. She found a spell that I could use to bind you here."

Callia turns to Brock, rage simmering in her dark gaze. "You killed my brothers and sisters. You all did. You massacred us out of fear, and then your mother killed me to hide her secret. You all deserved your fates."

Brock frowns. "Hate begets hate. Violence begets violence. I could justify what we did by pointing out what your people did to an entire generation of our eggs. And maybe you could go back further and argue we deserved that. Does it matter? If we continue this path there will be no more of either of our kind left."

Callia spits. "There are no more unicorns left. I was the last one."

I point to Ana. "There is her. She is part of you and part of the dragons, yet you would use her as a weapon to murder? A child? Your child?"

Callia's face drops as she sees her daughter, truly sees her. Ana's eyes have returned to normal and she looks as she truly is, a little girl who is lost, alone, and scared. And tortured by the memories of what she has done under the control of someone else.

"Gods, what have I done to you my child? What have I done?"

Callia drops to her knees. "Most of them are dead and yet I feel no relief. No hope. No peace. I am stuck forever in this hell Amora sent me to when I would not let her kill our daughter."

Brock turns to Callia. "I am tired of the wars. Of the fighting. Of the killing. We will not be friends. And it will take me lifetimes to forgive what you have done to my family. Just as it will take you lifetimes to forgive me for what I've done to yours. But perhaps we can try? For our children's sake?"

Callia's eyes flick to the side, shame filling her face.

"I do not know how to stop, but I agree, the bloodshed cannot continue. Vengeance has not given me what I'd hoped, but neither will forgiveness, I fear. I am too lost for both."

She turns to me. "What will you do to me now? Where will I go?"

"Where you deserve," I say softly.

THE PUNISHMENT

"If you are seeking, seek us with joy
    For we live in the kingdom of joy.
    Do not give your heart to anything else
    But to the love of those who are clear joy,
    Do not stray into the neighborhood of despair.
    For there are hopes: they are real, they exist –
    Do not go in the direction of darkness –
    I tell you: suns exist."
    ~Rumi

THE TENSION between Callia and Brock is thick, and with the dragons leaving this world and the unicorns extinct, Ana is now all that's left of the two races, and none of us know what that will mean for her as she grows into her own powers—if she has any left at all.

Only time will tell what the future holds for the child.

We stand by the ocean near the castle, the five Night brothers, myself, Ana, Brock and Zara, and Lilith who has just arrived.

Callia awaits her fate nervously.

"Are you sure this will work?" I ask Lilith, for the umpteenth time.

"Yes," she says with slight exasperation. "I obtained this spell from a solid source."

It is meant to open the door to the world of spirits, but I'm nervous as I begin the incantation. So much could go wrong. The last thing I want to do is create a tear in the fabric of reality and unleash the undead into the Otherworld.

We just narrowly avoided an end of world scenario. We don't need a ghost apocalypse now.

But we have to do something with Callia. She can't stay in this world as she is. She's a risk to others and she cannot heal while living in limbo.

The Night brothers stand near me and I channel their power with mine as I speak the ancient words. They are unfamiliar on my tongue, but Lilith and Brock both helped me learn the proper pronunciation.

As I speak, my hands begin to glow and a streak of light and darkness woven together spreads, creating a portal that peels open, and producing a window into the realm of the dead.

"It is time," I say to Callia.

I could force her into the portal, but I remain hopeful that won't be necessary. It will be better for her own soul's journey if she steps in on her own.

She looks around, fear etched in her face.

She has clung to hatred and revenge for so long, she knows nothing else.

Brock can barely look at her, but as Callia takes a step forward, something within the portal shifts as a green landscape of rolling hills comes into focus. And then I see them.

Hundreds of unicorns prancing and playing. One gallops over to the portal and shifts into a beautiful woman with deep mahogany hair and matching skin. She peers through, as if looking into a dream, and then she drops to her knees. "My Queen."

Callia startles, then steps forward, reaching out a hand. "Lumara? Is that really you?"

Tears stream down both their faces as the Queen of the Unicorns steps through the portal and joins her people after millennia apart. They take hands and walk towards the others. When they reach the glade, they shift into their unicorn forms and Callia is surrounded by her people.

Brock's face is hard, impassive, as she watches this, and I can only imagine what she's thinking or feeling. Callia, who killed her siblings, now gets to be with her kind. And Brock is alone.

I glance at Lilith, who seems to read my mind and nods.

I concentrate and the scene shifts to one of mountain tops and endless skies. And five dragons flying against the backdrop of a beautiful, warm sun. Brock gasps and moves closer. "My family," she says, softly.

"Would you like to speak with them?" I ask.

She reaches her hand out, nearly touching the portal, her eyes misting over. "Can I?"

I nod and move away from the gateway so she has some time alone with her siblings.

I take this moment to enjoy the crashing of the waves against the shore, and Cole joins me, his arm sliding around my waist.

"Are you coming to say goodbye again?" I ask without looking at him.

I've been in fear of this moment since the battle with Amora. He saved us, saved the world, by showing up. I couldn't have done that spell without him. Without all five of them. When I expanded the lands here, I was building on what already existed. I had enough power to do that. But this time, it was different. I had to stop the destruction of the Otherworld, which basically meant rebuilding it from within. I needed every element amplified to accomplish that. Cole was integral in that.

Since then he's stayed, though he is often missing for long periods. Each time, I expect he won't come back, but he does.

But I've been waiting for the final goodbye.

And here it is.

He moves to stand in front of me, his dark gaze capturing mine. "I've spoken to my brothers," he says softly, his lilting French accent like music. "And if it's all right with you, I'd like to stay."

My eyes widen. "For good?"

He nods. "Forever."

Tears blur my vision and I hug him fiercely. "Of course it's okay with me," I say. "We are all meant to be together."

We walk hand in hand back to the portal and Brock is saying her final goodbyes. Ava'Kara is there in human form, gazing longingly at her daughter. When she sees me, she smiles. "You have done well, my friend. This world is in the best of hands with you."

After saying her last goodbyes, Brock turns to face us with tears in her eyes. "We must go now. My world awaits."

We've already said our goodbyes, but we exchange one last hug and watch as they fly into the sky through the tear Brock opens. When it closes behind them, I sigh and turn to finish sealing the portal I created into the world of the dead.

But just as I'm about to, Lilith puts a hand on mine. "There's one more who wants to come through," she says, her gaze distant.

I wait, watching as the portal shifts once again and standing by a cottage is... Adam.

I cry out, and step closer, wanting desperately to go through and hug him once more. Cole takes my hand to keep me in this world as Adam moves closer to the doorway. "Evie," he says softly, his big blue eyes so achingly familiar. "I am so sorry I left you the way I did."

Tears stream down my face. "Oh, Adam. I wish you were here," I say. "I would give anything for you to be back with me."

"It's all okay, sis," he says. "I'm healing. My heart and soul are healing. And someday I will come back to you. Someday we will be together again. Just know, I'm safe. And I'll love you forever. It's always going to be you and me against the world."

"See you soon, then," I say. "I'll be looking for you."

He smiles. "We will always find each other. We always have."

And then he is gone.

EPILOGUE

"This is love: to fly toward a secret sky, to cause a hundred veils to fall each moment. First, to let go of life. Finally, to take a step without fear."
~Rumi
1 year later

LILY AND KAYA gaze deeply into each other's eyes as they take their vows to one another. We are in the center of the majestic grove surrounded by trees. They are both dressed in full dryad style, with wildflowers and vines flowing from their beautiful gowns.

Alina, barely walking, totters nearby, with Moon to keep her steady, and she randomly tosses rose petals at people.

All our friends are here to celebrate the mating of these remarkable dryads.

"I now give to you the beautiful mating of Lily and Kaya, forever bound by love, by respect, by compassion, and by the elements that shape our world."

They kiss and our friends cheer, tossing flowers at the happy couple.

The ceremony was short and sweet, but the after-party will last all night, as is tradition.

There are tables set up with drink and food, mats for resting when people need to, and music for dancing. It is festive and lighthearted, and everyone we care about is here.

This last year has brought so much change to the Otherworld. A new form of government, rebuilding areas that were destroyed by Amora, and a shift in the way everything is managed.

It hasn't been easy. Many have been resistant to change. But slowly we are showing people that the best way to move forward is actually going forwards, not backwards. We can no longer live in the past if we want a world where everyone is safe and happy.

Ana comes over to me carrying two drinks and hands me one. "It was beautiful," she says shyly.

She is still coming out of her shell, and her healing will take time. But she is finally excited to start school with other kids her age.

I watch as the Gargoyle's daughter plays with Alina. The Ifrits join them, their new baby in hand. He's six months old now and already bursting into flames at random times. Alina loves him and is one of the few kids who can actually hold him without injury. Fortunately, the Gargoyle's child is immune to fire as well, being stone and all.

Lily and Kaya dance in blissful synchronicity, swaying to the music, lost in their love.

Lilith comes to me, a smile on her lips. "Will there be a wedding in your future?" she asks.

I laugh. "I'm not entirely sure what the logistics would be to marry five men at once," I say. "But I think our bonds are pretty well established without all this."

This year has brought a lot of personal healing to our family. The Nights and Matilda have sorted through their complicated history. The brothers have had ups and downs with Cole, but all in all we've made it work.

Lilith moves on, to chat with others, and Cole joins me. "Did I hear something about a wedding?" he asks.

I slide an arm through his. "I don't think we need one to make what we have count, do you?"

He looks down at a me. "No, but there is something I wanted to talk to you about. I want to bind myself to you, as part of the Order of Druids," he says softly.

I pause. This is huge for him. We've never talked about it. I've never demanded it. With what Cole went through, I never expected it, to be honest. "Are you sure?"

He nods. "It's the one piece missing, and I want that with you. Only you."

"Do your brothers know?" I ask.

"I wanted you to be the first, but I'll tell them."

I hold him back. "Not today. Let today be about Lily. We have plenty of time."

That night there is much celebration, laughter and joy, and as I take turns dancing with each of the brothers, I'm reminded of just how lucky I am to have them in my life. They each bring a special kind of magic to my heart. Not just their elemental magic, but their soul magic, that connection that fills me and makes me feel like I've finally found home.

Elijah matches my intellect. Pushes me to new knowledge and understanding. I can stay up all night talking and reading with him. He shares my passion for books like none other.

Derek makes me laugh, soothes over hurt feelings with his calming water magic and verbally spars with me.

Liam is my fire. He burns as hot as I do and fans the flames of my passion, in and out of the bedroom. He is my music and my warmth.

Cole... Cole helps me to embrace my shadow self, the light and the dark within me. He shows me how to hold the duality of my nature together in a way that makes me stronger.

And Sebastian... he is my rock, my foundation, the man I know will hold me up when I need extra strength. He supports me and loves me through it all.

These men together create the family I have craved

my whole life. They form the unbreakable circle in which I stand.

THE NEXT DAY I have a job interview. Not for myself, of course, but for a new assistant for The Night Firm.

It has to be held at the courthouse, since our castle is still full of people celebrating Lily's wedding.

I'm sitting at my desk when she arrives, and I have her escorted in.

"I'm Kass," she says smiling.

She's a beautiful woman with a scanty resume and I've been curious about her since reviewing her application.

"Tell me why you want to work for the Night Firm," I say.

She hesitates. "I... I've only been in this world a short time, and I'm still trying to figure out where I belong. I was recently turned into a vampire and most of my human life was wasted on... well, let's just say I didn't have that great of an upbringing or even direction, really. I know the Night Firm is no longer a legal defense, but is now about making sure the disenfranchised of the world get equal access to resources and opportunities. I want to be a part of that. I want this new life to matter. To make a difference. I know I don't have experience, but I'm a fast learner and I will work hard, I promise you that."

I study the woman before me. She and I are very different in many ways. She's less polished, less educated than I was when I came to the Firm. But she has the same haunted look in her eyes I did. A look that speaks of pain and loss. Like me, she needs a new path that will give her life meaning.

Before I can comment, she shifts uncomfortably. "I understand if I'm not a fit... or if, if the Night brothers won't want me."

She may not be the perfect fit on paper, and it might be complicated, all things considered, but my flash buzzes and I know what I must do. I stand and offer her my hand. "Welcome to the Night Firm."

THE END

For a dark, delicious and deadly spin off standalone romance, check out WANTED and find out happened to a key character in this series once he left! Keep reading for a chapter teaser of this novel.

ABOUT WANTED

From USA Today bestselling author Karpov Kinrade and Liv Chatham comes a dark love story that will break you and remake you.

IT STARTS with a help wanted ad.

The mysterious man who just bought the grandest mansion in town needs a housekeeper.

No one's met him.

No one knows who he is.

I'm about to find out that he's much more than he appears.

Everyone has skeletons in their closest.

His are just more literal than most.

I didn't expect to fall for him.

I didn't expect to feel the way I do when I'm with him.

And though his skeletons are gruesome, mine are the ones that will end up destroying us both.

My new boss only has three rules, and I break them all the day I start working for him.

This isn't a love story, though you might wish it were.

This is a survival story, with love the cost of admission.

And death the price for betrayal.

THIS IS a complete standalone dark romance / paranormal romance for fans of Leia Stone, HM Ward, K.F. Breene, Shannon Mayer and Bella Forrest. Includes potentially triggering themes of drug and domestic abuse.

AND for more epic reverse harem romance, check out
Dungeon Queen on Amazon.

WANTED: CHAPTER 1

I'm recording everything that happens in the very likely scenario that my whole plan goes to shit and all that's left to tell the story is this journal. If you're reading this, I'm probably dead, and it's too late to do anything about any of it now. But, at least, you'll know the truth. And I won't hold back. I won't try to make myself look better than I am. I have no delusions about myself.

I began the day stealing from a department store and ended with lying to my new boss.

I'm no saint, but I'm far from the worst that exists. No, there are much worse specimens of humanity than me. They're the ones to be afraid of and the kind I'm trying to get away *from*. But I don't think it's going to work.

After all, nothing in my life has ever worked.

I'm not trying to wallow in self-pity. I'm just being honest. Some lives shine with a kind of preternatural luck that follows them around. Others live under a perpetual storm cloud.

My life is the latter.

But who knows, maybe the weather is turning in my favor for once.

You never know, right?

***

STEAL a little and they'll jail your ass, steal a lot and they'll make you queen. It's a Bob Dylan quote with my personal spin on a few of the words. And it's all I could think about as I walked casually through the exit of the department store with new as-yet-paid-for dress and shoes shoved into my oversized purse.

It was only a borrow. I'll return them tomorrow.

However, stores generally frown on you taking their shit without paying, so I schooled my face into a bored housewife expression and causally browsed a few items lining the back of the store on my way out.

Why do they put shit past the checkout stands? You don't pass them when you come in, only when you go out, and by then you've already paid. What's the point?

Fortunately for me, the store alarm didn't go off. No one tried to stop me. In fact, one of the employees nodded his head in my direction with a smile as I left. "Have a nice day," he said with a wink. "And come back again soon."

He looked college-aged, with a sweet grin and kind brown eyes.

"Thanks," I said blandly, not giving into the temptation to flirt back.

He was cute and it could have been fun, but he looked too innocent to handle the skeletons piling up in my closet. And by the time this blistering summer is over, there will be more.

I sighed deeply once I was safely in my beaten-up old car, doors closed and locked, air conditioning drying the sweat dotting my skin.

I studied my hands gripping the steering wheel as

they shook, my fingernails bitten down to stumps, my cuticles in need of some serious TLC. You'd think this was my first time stealing, the way my heart fluttered in my chest like a hummingbird on crack.

Closing my eyes, I steadied myself with a few deep breaths.

A sharp knock on the window startled me back to the present and scared the living hell out of me.

It was the cute store guy.

Jesus.

I rolled down my window and put on my best 'polite but I'm in a hurry' smile. "Is something wrong?"

If I got caught, I'd be ruined, and I wouldn't be the only one to suffer.

He held up a cell phone. "I think you left this in the store?"

With a relieved sigh, I took it from him, feeling twice the idiot. How could I be so stupid? "Thank you. It must've fallen from my purse."

This time, my smile was one hundred percent genuine. Losing my phone would have been Bad-with-a-capital-B.

He glanced inside my car, towards said purse, but fortunately, I'd zipped it shut, the stolen items safely tucked out of sight.

"Hey, so, I was wondering..." he began.

I inwardly cringed, just knowing what was next. Could I start the car and hightail it out there fast enough? *Would* I?

Then, he stunned me with a nervous slur of, "Would you like to grab a coffee after my shift?"

I blinked. "Thanks, but I have a job interview today." This was it? Really?

His smile faltered. "Oh, right. Well, good luck."

Before he could ask for my number, I rolled up my window, waved, and then drove off.

A quick glance in the rearview mirror revealed him standing there, a bit forlorn. He watched my car leave the lot before he turned back toward the store.

"Your lucky day, bud," I muttered under my breath.

Boys like troubled girls before they know what kind of trouble they're really in for. I'd just saved him a shit ton of heartache.

My phone binged just as I pulled up to the curb and parked in front of my house. I already knew who it was, and a blanket of depression dropped over me as I checked the messages, proving myself right.

ARE YOU READY?

WITH SHAKING HANDS, I replied.

YES.

. . .

GOOD.

I SAT THERE, waiting for the three dots to blink, signaling a reply, but when nothing appeared on the tiny screen, I felt the anger beginning to bubble. That was it? That was all I was going to get? I mentally screamed a few choice words at the sender of the texts, then grabbed my purse and headed into the house.

I heard the sound of an argument even before I set foot on the cracked concrete steps. One kick of the screen door later, I was in the living room, tense and ready.

My father, a tall brute of a man with beady eyes, a rounded stomach fed by liquor, and meaty fists, towered over my little brother, wielding a broken beer bottle like a knife.

"You do as you're told," he was shouting. "Or I'll shove this so far up your ass you'll be eating glass and shit for a *week*."

My little brother stood there, trembling, with his thin forearm protecting his face. At fourteen, he was small for his age and much preferred reading books to fighting.

As my father lurched forward to backhand my brother, I shoved Jeremy aside and stepped between them.

The blow jarred my teeth and pain exploded across my cheekbone. If there weren't any broken bones, I'd be shocked. I choked, clutching my face as tears stung my eyes.

My dad's eyes widened. "What are you doing, you little slut?" He snarled, sending spittle straight at me. "You're nothing but a worthless whore." He stumbled to the couch to grab another beer.

Now was my chance, before he could wind himself up for another strike, a strike I sure as hell wasn't going to be around to take. I grabbed Jeremy by the arm and dragged him out of the room to our shared bedroom at the end of the hall before that blow could land.

Once locked in the safety of our shared bedroom, I checked him over quickly. "Are you okay? Did he hurt you?"

Jeremy shook his head, but tears glistened in his large eyes.

My heart broke and I pulled him close, hugging him tight. "I'll get us out of this. I promise." And I would get us out, by any means necessary, even if it involved me dying.

My little brother's shoulders shook in mute sobs, silent as they must be in this house. We are the children of the silent pain. I grimaced. If nothing else, Children of the Silent Pain would be a cool band name.

When he calmed down, I released him and wiped his face with my sleeve. "I have to go, but you should climb out the window and stay at Rick's tonight. Go to school with him in the morning."

Jeremy's caramel eyes widened. "But won't you get in trouble if I leave?"

"I'll be fine. Don't worry about me. I can take care of myself," I said. We are twelve years apart, and I only came back to this hell hole to rescue him. Well... mostly for him. I had a plan. Kind of. I shoved him toward the window. "Now, go!"

He nodded and detoured to grab his backpack, then returned to the window and climbed out.

I exhaled and turned my attention back to my father. He had the TV in the living room on as loud as it could go and now, he was bellowing at the game.

Hoping he'd remain distracted, I crept down the hall and snuck into the kitchen with as much stealth as I could muster. After snagging a bag of frozen peas from the freezer and grabbing the ibuprofen, I scuttled back to my bedroom and locked the door.

Suddenly drained, I collapsed on my bed and then slid to the floor, pressing the frozen peas to my cheek.

I tried to cry.

I wanted to cry.

Hell, I *needed* to cry.

But... nothing. I felt dead inside—and that scared me more than anything.

I needed to feel. *Do* something to numb the pain that shriveled my soul, made me feel like I was a shell of a person, already dead, a ghost of myself haunting my own life.

I felt under my bed until my fingers tripped over

the small silver box that held a razor blade and alcohol wipes. Still numb, I pulled it out and flipped open the lid. It took only a second to clean the blade, and then, I was pulling my shorts up as far as I could, eyeing the small white scars crisscrossing my inner thighs.

With a deep breath, I pressed the metal blade into my flesh, gently at first, then with more pressure until I felt the skin brake under that sharp edge of pain.

Crimson blood spilled and dripped down my pale leg.

Relief surged through me, almost as if the seeping blood released the poison lurking in my soul. I sighed as the tears finally began to fall.

I'm not proud of it, and I'm not writing for sympathy. But I promised I wouldn't paint myself in a false, flattering light, and I'm keeping my word—at least, in this instance.

Carefully, I cleaned myself with an alcohol wipe, applied a bandage, and then shoved the container back under my bed.

It was time to move on. I had an interview. I opened my purse and grabbed my 'borrowed' outfit, a conservative navy-blue, button-up dress with matching slip-on ballet shoes. Everything fit to a T and minutes later, I stood in front of the mirror, staring at the image reflected there.

"Not bad," I murmured. No, I looked damn good. Striking, even. The color brought out the blue in my eyes and complemented my dark hair and fair skin. Of course, I could still see the tattoos on my arms, but as practically everyone had them these days, I didn't see how that would be a problem.

Then, I glanced at my cheek and winced outright at the dramatic array of reds and blues standing out against my white skin in a nice bruise despite the ice and meds.

It took a good twenty minutes to do my makeup, thanks to the purple spreading over my cheekbone. I flinched each time I dabbed on the concealer, but finally, I'd finished and even I couldn't tell I'd been hit. I just had to keep my fingers crossed that my eye wouldn't swell. Then, there'd be no hiding my injury.

After one last dab of lip gloss, I followed my brother's path and shimmied through the window. I made it back to my car and then I was off again, before my father knew I'd even left.

It was dusk by the time I reached the address for my interview. I switched off the engine and settled in my car, preparing to wait, as instructed, until full darkness descended.

I didn't mind. It gave me the chance to study the mansion I'd be cleaning, provided I got the job, of course.

The place was massive, by far the largest and remotest estate in and around our small town. A forest of trees blanketed the mansion from the road and you had to drive down a long, winding driveway before you'd even catch a glimpse of the slate tile roof. It wasn't until the last bend, when you were upon the place that you got a good view.

Other than the ornately carved tall, black double arched front door, the mansion was entirely white with stately columns that gave it a Roman villa vibe. Fountains graced the lawn and a meticulous garden of red roses lined the walkway from the drive to the front door.

For a place that had been vacant forever, it looked remarkably well kept. The man who'd bought it last month was a mystery in our small Northern California town. No one had seen him, but everyone had heard the rumors of his wealth and that he'd paid for the place in cash. With that kind of money, he had to be dripping with diamonds. He'd have to be to buy the place. Few could afford it, and those who could didn't want it after... well, after everything went down. A real estate agent is required by law to disclose when a murder's been committed on a property. That typically doesn't help sell a place.

I sat in my car, tapping a beat on the steering wheel as I watched and waited. Finally, the sun sank out of view and when the full moon hung over the treetops, fully visible, I checked my phone and scanned the job details one last time.

Job details. Check. Like I hadn't had them memorized already. Well, there was nothing left to do but get the show on the road.

Inhaling a deep breath, I exited my car and walked

to the entrance. After lifting the brass knocker and giving the door a sharp rap, I rubbed my sweating palms against my thigh without thinking. Damnit. I'd just left a dark wet smudge on the borrowed dress.

I drew a deep breath and glanced around. I'd been here, at the house, once before, but it wasn't a night I liked to recall.

Fortunately, the door opened, sparing me the memories, and I straightened my spine and tried to act like someone else. Someone poised, polished, and well-spoken. Someone who deserved to scrub the toilets of the filthy rich.

A tall, rail thin man wearing a traditional butler uniform greeted me. "You must be Miss Kassandra Blackwood," he said as he ushered me inside. "Welcome."

"Thanks... er...thank you," I replied, belatedly polishing my speech so I could later polish the silver here.

My phone buzzed in my purse, and I scowled at the annoyance.

The butler's eyes flicked down, but he said nothing. Instead, he escorted me to a small room a few doors to the left of the foyer and offered me a seat on a plush leather chair. "Please, wait a moment. The Count will be right with you."

Count? I raised an eyebrow. Had he said...Count? Just who the hell *was* this guy? I scanned the room assessing the value of the rugs, furniture, and knickknacks in a cursory calculation. It didn't take long to determine that, most likely, just one of the knickknacks on his shelf was worth more than my whole life. I couldn't imagine being so wealthy that you'd spend insane amounts of money on painted eggs or some shit just to display them behind locked glass doors. It was vulgar.

But who was I to judge? After all, I didn't have two pennies to rub together.

Then, the butler returned, and I stood as he smiled and gestured for me to follow. "Right this way."

He led me through gilded hallways with more molding than wall, and past rooms filled to the brim with priceless antiques. Obviously, the Count had changed a lot about the house since I'd been there last.

Finally, the butler escorted me into an office lined wall-to-wall with leather-bound books. The room was dark and very Gothic, without windows. The only sources of light were the ornate iron candelabras, each boasting five beeswax pillar candles. Strange. The room was an odd choice considering the rest of the mansion had electricity.

Under any other circumstances, I'd have hightailed it out of there. The whole place screamed sexual-assault-that-gets-thrown-out-of-court—that is, if it ever made to court in the first place with me. After all, they'd take one look at how I'm dressed and then another at my past and conclude I'd clearly asked for it.

Yet the more I inspected the place, the more the

highly tuned street-smart side of me kept telling the rest of me to calm down, that it wasn't getting any real rapey vibes.

I hesitated, on the fence, but deep inside, I knew I couldn't just walk away. I didn't have a choice.

Trusting the street-smarts knew what they were talking about, I stepped inside.

Immediately, the butler left, closing the door behind him with a click.

It was then I saw the man, standing in the shadows. As I watched, he emerged into the circle of candlelight, book in hand.

It took a moment for my eyes to adjust to the lighting, but when they did, my jaw dropped.

He was tall, at least 6'3", and elegantly lean in a black suit tailored to his trim, muscular frame. Yet it was his face that drew my gaze, so fine, ageless, and all chiseled angles. His dark, nearly black, eyes glinted in the candlelight or perhaps with a hint of madness.

He looked so elegant, suave, and fierce all at once.

He snapped his book shut and set it on a nearby shelf, his gaze never once leaving mine. "Good evening, Miss Blackwood," he said as he reached out his hand in greeting.

A shiver ran up my spine the instant our hands met, and almost at once, a wave of unexpected desire rolled over me, making my legs tremble and taking me by surprise. Shocked, I drew a silent, fortifying breath and stood firm, willing myself not to flinch under his gaze or touch. "Thank you for the interview, Mr. ...?" I never got a name. Just an address.

He tilted his head, causing a lock of dark hair to fall across his forehead as his long, elegant fingers tightened ever so slightly around my hand. "It's Count... actually."

I narrowed my eyes. "That's rather grandiose," I teased and then promptly bit my lip. *Don't freaking forget your place, Kass.*

Fortunately, he didn't appear offended, judging by the wry smile that curved his lips, anyway. "It is a title well-earned," he said mildly. Then, his eyes dropped to my hand, still clutched in his, and I stared at the line of his thick, black lashes as he studied the ink on my arm.

Suddenly self-conscious, I pulled free of his grasp. Instantly, part of me felt a loss at the lack of contact, which was, of course, a shit-ton of pure stupidness, so I mentally clocked myself in the head, hoping to knock some sense into my brain.

"Please, sit," the Count waved a hand at a tufted leather chair as he took the seat behind the mahogany desk nearby. "Tell me, Kassandra. May I call you Kassandra?"

To be perfectly honest, the way he said my name made me a bit lightheaded. I sat down, mentally kicking myself again and forced my mind back to the interview. For the first time, I realized he'd never actually told me his name, but now it felt weird to ask again. "My friends call me Kass," I said, clearing my throat. "But Kassandra is fine too."

"Tell me, Kassandra, why are you applying for this job?"

This was it, my moment to shine. I looked him straight in the eye and recited from memory the script I'd been given to say, "I'm passionate about house-keeping and finding new and innovative ways to keep a home clean and inviting. I'm organized, strong, and can work long hours without tiring." Ha! What a crock. "I would be an asset to any house." There, I'd nailed every word *and* emotion.

The Count leaned back, steepled his fingers, and studied me in the candlelight. The flickering of flames lent him a menacing look but strangely, that only somehow amplified the attraction I felt. This wasn't an innocent boy who didn't know which way was up. This was a man... a man who had clearly walked with dark-ness and lived to tell the tale—and a man who obvi-ously knew his way around a woman, maybe even women with my kind of demons. My libido warmed at that, a libido that had been very much neglected of late due to my inability to make good decisions on the men front. Yet, while I was a year into taking a sabbatical from men entirely, my libido whispered I just might want to make an exception for *this* tall drink of water.

Then, I became suddenly aware of the silence hanging heavy in the room and the fact that the Count was just sitting there, watching me.

I gritted my teeth. *Quit thinking with your pants and think with your head, Kass.*

As if aware I was suddenly paying attention again, the Count arched a cool brow and said in a low, menacing voice, "I have three rules for anyone who works with me or lives with me, Kassandra."

I froze as a prickle of foreboding crept down my neck.

"The first rule, Kassandra, is no lying. Ever. Without exception. So, before I terminate this interview and have you escorted out, I will give you one more chance to answer my question. Why are you applying for this job? This time, I want the truth."

He never raised his voice, but there was such power behind his words I felt compelled to obey, and that terrified the ever-loving shit out of me.

This was the moment I should have gotten the hell out of there. But I didn't. I couldn't.

Still, I needed to know what I was playing with, so I asked, "And what are the other two rules?"

His dark brows creased with displeasure. "We will go over those should you get the job."

It was my turn to frown. What a freaking strange interview. I sucked in a breath as I prepared a suitable combination of the truth. Then, I smiled, knowing exactly what I'd say. After all, a lie is always most believable when it contains a kernel of truth, and my lie had the advantage of being entirely true and entirely a lie at the exact same time.

"The truth is, I came back home after being gone for some time to help take care of my little brother after my mother died. I need a job, and this town isn't exactly overflowing with them. I'm a shit housekeeper and I couldn't care less about 'innovative cleaning techniques', but I *am* a hard worker and I will learn to do what you want and do it well, should you hire me." Let's see what he did with that. I raised an eyebrow at him as if to say, *"ball's in your court, buddy."*

He studied me for a long time. I didn't know if he was waiting for me to crack or what, but I didn't play his game. I just sat patiently, waiting. I could do that all night.

Finally, he smiled. It was brief, and it didn't reach his eyes entirely. Eyes that looked weighed down with so much pain it couldn't be hidden.

"Very well, Miss Blackwood, you're hired. You may move in tonight and start tomorrow."

"Thank you, I—" I paused as his words sank in. "Wait, what? Move in?"

He nodded. "Were you not aware? This is a live-in position. That's non-negotiable. Will that be a problem?"

I gulped. *Yes.* "No, not at all."

I plastered a smile on my face but inwardly I was already swearing at myself. *What the hell are you going to do now? You're really up shit creek, Kass.*

ABOUT THE AUTHOR

Karpov Kinrade is the pen name for the husband and wife writing duo of USA TODAY bestselling, award-winning authors Lux Karpov-Kinrade and Dmytry Karpov-Kinrade.

Together, they live in Ukiah, California and write fantasy and science fiction novels and screenplays, make music and direct movies.

Look for more from Karpov Kinrade in *The Night Firm, Vampire Girl, Of Dreams and Dragons, Nightfall Academy* and *Paranormal Spy Academy*. If you're looking for their suspense and romance titles, you'll now find those under Alex Lux.

They live with their three teens who share a genius for all things creative, and seven cats who think they rule the world (spoiler, they do.)

Want their books and music before anyone else and also enjoy weekly interactive flash fiction? Join them on Patreon at Patreon.com/karpovkinrade

Find them online at KarpovKinrade.com

On Facebook /KarpovKinrade

On Twitter @KarpovKinrade

And subscribe to their newsletter at ReadKK.com for special deals and up-to-date notice of new launches.

~~~~~

If you enjoyed this book, consider supporting the author by leaving a review wherever you purchased this book. Thank you.

ALSO BY KARPOV KINRADE

Dungeon Queen

Warrior Queen

The Night Firm

I Am the Wild

I Am the Storm

I Am the Night

Wanted

In the Vampire Girl Universe

Vampire Girl

Vampire Girl 2: Midnight Star

Vampire Girl 3: Silver Flame

Vampire Girl 4: Moonlight Prince

Vampire Girl 5: First Hunter

Vampire Girl 6: Unseen Lord

Vampire Girl 7: Fallen Star

Vampire Girl: Copper Snare

Vampire Girl: Crimson Cocktail

Vampire Girl: Christmas Cognac

Of Dreams and Dragons

Get the soundtrack for I AM THE WILD, OF DREAMS AND DRAGONS and MOONSTONE ACADEMY wherever music can be found.

<u>Nightfall Academy</u>

Court of Nightfall

Weeper of Blood

House of Ravens

Night of Nyx

Song of Kai

Daughter of Strife

Paranormal Spy Academy (complete academy sci fi thriller romance)

<u>Forbidden Mind</u>

<u>Forbidden Fire</u>

<u>Forbidden Life</u>

Our ALEX LUX BOOKS!

<u>The Seduced Saga (paranormal romance with suspense)</u>

Seduced by Innocence

Seduced by Pain

Seduced by Power

Seduced by Lies

Seduced by Darkness

The Call Me Cat Trilogy (romantic suspense)

Call Me Cat

Leave Me Love

Tell Me True

(Standalone romcon with crossover characters)

Hitched

Whipped

Kiss Me in Paris (A standalone romance)

Our Children's Fantasy collection under Kimberly Kinrade

The Three Lost Kids series

Lexie World

Bella World

Maddie World

The Three Lost Kids and Cupid's Capture

The Three Lost Kids and the Death of the Sugar Fairy

The Three Lost Kids and the Christmas Curse

Made in the USA
Coppell, TX
28 April 2021

54657072R00154